MW01138213

Jim Tully, 1886–1947

SHANTY IRISH

BY

Jim Tully

Edited by Paul J. Bauer and Mark Dawidziak
Foreword by John Sayles

Black Squirrel Books
KENT, OHIO

Library of Congress Catalog Card Number 2009000937

ISBN 978-1-60635-023-2

Manufactured in the United States of America

First published by Albert & Charles Boni, Inc., 1928.

Library of Congress Cataloging-in-Publication Data

Tully, Jim.
    Shanty Irish / by Jim Tully ; edited by Paul J. Bauer and Mark
Dawidziak ; foreword by John Sayles.
        p. cm.
    ISBN 978-1-60635-023-2 (pbk. : alk. paper) ∞
    1. Irish Americans—Fiction. I. Bauer, Paul, 1956– II. Dawidziak,
Mark, 1956– III. Title.
    PS3539.U44S5 2009
    813'.52—dc22

                                                          2009000937

British Library Cataloging-in-Publication data are available.

13 12 11 10 09   5 4 3 2 1

To
MARNA

CONTENTS

[vii]

CONTENTS

There is in the human intellect a power of expansion—I might almost call it a power of creation—which is brought into play by the simple brooding upon facts.

TYNDALL.

FOREWORD
John Sayles

"I developed early a capacity for remembered sorrow."

Jim Tully stands out in American literature as one of the few realist writers who did not just visit the rougher environs of human experience for material, but was fully *of* those depths (poverty, orphanage, menial labor, jail, the boxing ring, and the carnival) and somehow survived to tell the tale. The shanty Irish and hard-luck regular joes in his stories are always just smart enough to be aware of their own ignorance, and to dream (most often fueled by whiskey) scenarios of a beauty and import they know they will never experience. These are the homeless characters I used to see, chilly days on the the road, taking refuge in public libraries throughout the country, the ones not sleeping face down on an open book but reading, the text as likely to be Dostoevsky as Zane Grey. I had more literary discussions with stone alcoholics working day labor jobs than I ever had at college, the gist of the conversation never about where a book stood in the canon of Western writing but about the lives of the characters and what understanding could be drawn from them, "It's nice to know I'm not the only failure in the world," I heard from a shaky-handed shovel jockey who'd just plowed through all of the works of Theodore Dreiser, "and far from the worst."

Jim Tully wrote like a man surprised to still be breathing, thinking, feeling. He had access to books growing up, ten-cent paperbacks passed on from his emotionally mute, ditch digging father, and more importantly he had the heritage of the Irish tongue, which, once the Empire's language was imposed on the island, retained the poetic rhythm and graphic hyperbole of Gaelic.

> "Tim Walsh came to me father's house. 'Shake hands wit' a murderer,' says he to the ould man. An' me father says, 'Who did ye murder,' says he, an' Tim says, 'Who could I be murderin'? Why the Blakes—father an' son. . . . '
>
> "'It's too bad,' says me father, 'ye should o' killed his three brothers. . . . '
>
> "'Give me time,' says Tim Walsh."

English, yes, but never the King's English.

Jim Tully's shanty Irish are not the sentimental, winking, top o' the morning Barry Fitzgerald tipplers of vaudeville stage and silver screen; these are the people forbidden by law in early New York to congregate in groups larger than three, the original foreign menace, depicted in newspaper cartoons as simian-browed bog-trotters, militant Catholics who despise priests and observe more than a few pagan Celtic superstitions and rituals. Tully's people never hooked onto the steady ladder of civil service like so many Irish (my own family included) city dwellers—they lived in the rural swamps of Ohio, grubbing a living out of land that nobody else wanted. But some of them, especially his grandfather, Old Hughie, who is the soul of this book, can imagine a different world. Like much of Irish folklore it is an exaggerated land of giants and great feats of strength and angels polishing the stars with their wings, but there is ever a dark river of resentment and discontent flowing through the discourse.

"It is of the famine I'm talkin' whin the dumb Irish wint starvin' to glory, wit' the praists showin' thim how to die like Christians gnawin' at the wood of the cross."

[xiii]

In this book Tully makes no attempt to craft an adventure, or even a narrative of his upbringing as his predecessor Jack London did with his own desperate beginnings. He presents a series of family stories, their order only roughly chronological, with none of the striving for literature one finds in Hamlin Garland or other refugee/reporters from the unexamined life. "If you are going to understand me," he seems to be saying, "you must know these people."

Some of the cultural malaise is familiar from the *Dubliners* of James Joyce, but those Irish are petty bourgeoisie city-dwellers back on the drizzly, socially pinched island. Tully's people are simple laborers in the open air of America, where there is thought to be no ceiling on success. They live in the woods, they dig in the dirt, they raise cattle and pigs (in fortunate times) and they drink. And drink. American boosterism and ambition seems not to have penetrated their consciousness; they bring a European fatalism to the New World. They take a stubborn, sometimes violent pride in being who they are (a religion that foresees the Eternal Lake of Fire for the mostly non-Catholic rich is a constant comfort) yet have few kind words to say about their brethren and revel in their feuds. "And they never spoke another word to each other for as long as they lived" is the last line of many an Irish family story—verbal exile, the withholding of talk, being the ultimate punishment. Jim Tully presents but does little to judge his relatives; he is still trying to figure them (and by extension, himself) out. The lesson his grandfather passes to him, again and again, is the importance of having no illusions, as if by expecting little or nothing he might never know disappointment.

Tully is a hard, rough nugget in the rich vein of American writing that leads to James T. Farrell and Nelson Algren, to the neighborhood elegies of *A Tree Grows in Brooklyn* or *Call It Sleep*. He ended up in Hollywood, of course, selling his own story and writing celebrity profiles of the vagabonds who had suddenly become world famous for what they did or looked like in front of a movie camera. *Shanty Irish* is a window, cracked and soiled, into a time and a place and a people before the moving pictures became an American obsession, people who had to create their own dreams, invent their own stories, and find escape from hopeless lives in hard liquor or the cold comfort of a promised Hereafter. That Jim Tully wrote at all was a miracle; that he wrote so well is a gift to the world.

INTRODUCTION
Paul J. Bauer and Mark Dawidziak

Jim Tully (June 3, 1886–June 22, 1947) was an American writer who won critical acclaim and commercial success in the 1920s and 30s. His rags-to-riches career may qualify him as the greatest long shot in American literature. Born near St. Marys, Ohio, to an Irish immigrant ditch-digger and his wife, Tully enjoyed a relatively happy but impoverished childhood until the death of his mother in 1892. Unable to care for him, his father sent him to an orphanage in Cincinnati. He remained there for six lonely and miserable years. What further education he acquired came in the hobo camps, boxcars, railroad yards, and public libraries scattered across the country. Finally, weary of the road, he arrived in Kent, Ohio, where he worked as a chainmaker, professional boxer, and tree surgeon. He also began to write, mostly poetry, which was published in the area newspapers.

Tully moved to Hollywood in 1912, when he began writing in earnest. His literary career took two distinct paths. He became one of the first reporters to cover Hollywood. As a free-lancer, he was not constrained by the studios and wrote about Hollywood celebrities (including Charlie Chaplin, for whom he had worked) in ways that they did not always find agreeable. For these pieces, rather tame by current standards, he became known as the most-feared man in Hollywood—a title he relished. Less lucrative, but closer to his heart, were the dark novels he wrote about his life on the road and the American underclass. He also wrote novels on prostitution, boxing, and Hollywood and a travel book. And there was *Shanty Irish*, a typically hard-edged yet affectionate memoir of his childhood. While some of the more graphic books ran afoul of the censors, they were also embraced by critics, including H. L. Mencken, George Jean Nathan, and Rupert Hughes. Tully, Hughes wrote, "has fathered the school of hard-boiled writing so zealously cultivated by Ernest Hemingway and lesser luminaries."

The literary path to *Shanty Irish* began with Tully drawing on his experiences of the road. Those roving years figure prominently in his first book, *Emmett Lawler* (1922), and his breakthrough work about hoboes, vagabonds, and road kids, *Beggars of Life* (1924). Tully's "road works" were followed by one of the earliest novels about Hollywood, *Jarnegan* (1926), and *Circus Parade* (1927), which recalled his youthful stints with a small circus in the South. Each of these four books charted a course that took Tully away, physically and emotionally, from his small Ohio hometown.

He reversed course, traveling back to his boyhood home for *Shanty Irish*, which he began writing in April of 1927. Published the following year, it is a sometimes-tragic, sometimes-hysterical chronicle of the people who had the most influence on his personality. They were the Tullys and, his mother's family, the Lawlers. Largely set in and around St. Marys, *Shanty Irish* is both an exploration and a celebration of his Irish-American family. It is also Jim Tully's most personal, lyrical, and humorous book.

The crisp phrasing and cold-eyed brutality of *Beggars of Life* and *Circus Parade* are again evident in *Shanty Irish*, yet it is in his fifth book that Tully gives freest reign to the sentimental, poetic side of his nature. Remarkably, the two disparate sides of the writer's nature never seem to be in conflict. They are, rather, in dynamic balance, the sardonic Irish rover's rough instincts tempered by those of the Irish poet.

Tully did not take up the ditch-digging profession of his father, also named Jim Tully, yet he digs deep into the soil of his native Ohio to describe what life was like in the late nineteenth century for a dirt-poor Irish-American family. The choice of subject doesn't seem all that startling today, but Tully was breaking new ground in the 1920s.

Although Irish immigrants were hired as manual laborers on canals and railroads well before the Great Potato Famine of the 1840s, their story had not yet been widely told. The Irish-American experience was first explored from the humorist's perspective in Chicagoan Finley Peter Dunne's Mr. Dooley books, published between 1898 and 1919. And Irish-American writers had made towering literary contributions before *Shanty Irish*. One need only mention Eugene O'Neill and F. Scott Fitzgerald. But neither Irish-American writer had yet set his sights on the Irish-American experience.

Blending humor and heartbreak, realism and lyricism, Tully's *Shanty Irish* anticipates the 1930s work of another Chicagoan, James T. Farrell. But where Farrell was interested in the experience of the Irish-American in the city, Tully's people are country and small town folk. Unlike Fitzgerald, who wrote so brilliantly about the riches and glamor of the Jazz Age, Tully was drawn to Gorky's lower depths—the underclass, the disadvantaged, the disenfranchised. Even though a proud Irish-American, Al Smith, ran for president the same year that *Shanty Irish* was published, America was not that far removed from the days of signs that declared, "No Irish need apply." Tully's parents toiled at the only work open to them: ditchers and domestics.

A book soaked in mud and whiskey, *Shanty Irish*, charts the Tully-Lawler journey from the horrors of the potato famine through the author's own childhood. His hard-drinking grandfather, old Hughie Tully, emerges as the book's most vividly drawn character, and his life and death frame the narrative. A constant presence in *Shanty Irish*, old Hughie spins yarns of Ireland, of his emigration, of his days traveling through the antebellum South as a lace "piddler," of "throwing dirt" for a living, of friends, and of enemies. Old Hughie is "capable of turning death into an Irish wake and pouring liquor down the throat of the corpse." *Shanty Irish*, though, is far from a one-grandfather show. It is, indeed, a book loaded with unforgettable characters.

Within the covers of this work, we meet the author's father, "a gorilla built" man whose stooped shoulders carry "the inherited burdens of a thousand dead Irish peasants." We meet his mother, Biddy, a "woman of imagination" who "had all the moods of April." We meet his uncle, ruthless John Lawler, tried, convicted, and sentenced to fifteen years in the Ohio penitentiary for stealing horses. We meet Aunt Moll, who shocks the family and the community by attempting to join the Walnut Grove Methodist Church. We meet the author's devoted older sister, Virginia, who inherits her mother's faith and mysticism.

These are not the Irish-American stereotypes that flourished on the vaudeville stage during the first twenty years of the 20th century or would populate so many Hollywood films in the 1930s. The author of *Shanty Irish* makes them distinctly Tully and distinctly Lawler. Yet through the prism of his family, he captures the shanty Irish-American experience. For all his rough-hewn sensibilities, Tully writes with perception and sensitivity about women, children, and the elderly.

At turns wry and raw, *Shanty Irish* manages to be both nostalgic and cynical. His use of irony is particularly sharp throughout, never more so than when describing the roistering Lawlers: "They were all devout Catholics during mass on Sundays." It's the type of terse turn of phrase that was a Mark Twain specialty. Perhaps there's an echo here of Twain's infamous line about "the serene confidence which a Christian feels in four aces."

With few words, Tully tells so much about his relatives. "At heart my father was an agnostic without knowing it," he writes. "His wife relied much on God. He did not interfere." He has, in three short sentences, defined their marriage, their beliefs, their understanding.

But Tully's memory also can be wonderfully journalistic in the precise details. Again recalling his father, Tully tells us:

He was nearsighted. When reading, he never moved his eyes. A country newspaper, a frayed volume of Shakespeare, or a medical almanac, it moved backward and forward within two inches of his left eye.

Tully inherited his father's love of reading and his agnosticism, but he also inherited a reluctance to judge friends and foes. Tully again echoes Twain when he discusses Virginia's devotion to Catholicism. "It rests me, and I feel better when I go to church," she says. "Even if in the end I find out I'm wrong I'd still think it was wiser to kid myself." Somewhere in there is Twain declaring that faith is believing what you know "ain't so." There's also, in Tully's acceptance of his sister's faith, something of Twain's rule that he should never undermine anyone's religion because those beliefs are of incalculable worth to that person. Given the Irish love of storytelling, it is not surprising that Tully spent his childhood immersed in family lore. And determined to render the Tullys and Lawlers as faithfully as possible, he visited his aging father in Dayton, Ohio, in August 1927 and began a correspondence in October. The letters, charming and sad, shed light on the two families' fortunes in America. For stories set in Ireland, there was no shortage of accounts of the famine. And in a small

1854 volume *Sketches of the Irish Bar* by Richard Lalor
Sheil, Tully found the story of John Walsh (changed
by Tully to Tim Walsh) which appears in the second
chapter of *Shanty Irish*. The story about the 1827
murder of a rent collector and its bloody aftermath
is drawn by Tully with little embellishment from
Sheil's account.

The question one always faces when reading Tully
is: How much is true? Tully opens *Shanty Irish* with a
clue. Hugh Tully is certainly the most memorable
character in all of Tully's books yet Jim was only fourteen when his grandfather died in 1900. And six of
young Jim's fourteen years were spent in an orphanage,
separated from his grandfather. While family members
could add a few stories to Jim's memories, much of
what Jim wrote about his grandfather came about
through the hard business of writing. When Jim pref-
aced *Shanty Irish* with a quote from the Irish physicist
John Tyndall (a move applauded by Mencken), he no
doubt had the creation of Hughie in mind.

There is in the human intellect a power of expansion—I might
almost call it a power of creation—which is brought into play
by the simple brooding upon facts.

Jim later recalled writing and rewriting the scene
that opens Chapter VIII. He originally wrote the
scene with Hughie and a "group of hospitable yokels"
sitting around a roaring fire one rainy night. When
Jim was unable to loosen his grandfather's tongue, he
tried a change of venue. Instead of a campfire, Jim
placed Hughie in a saloon. His writer's block was
broken with the introduction of a one-legged stranger
who walked through the swinging doors and pushed
the scene in a new direction. The barroom stories that
followed, Jim later wrote, came not from any particular memory but from "the simple brooding upon
facts" and the imagination, one might add, of a gifted
and unique writer.

As was his custom, Tully offered the chapters of
Shanty Irish to his trusted friend and critic, H. L.
Mencken, for possible inclusion in Mencken's *American Mercury*. Mencken, who could be gentle but
firm in declining work not up to his high standards,
snapped them up. Late 1927 to early 1928 was a very
productive period, with chapters of *Shanty Irish* and
film pieces pouring from his pen. There was the film-
ing of *Beggars of Life* and a considerable amount of
time spent advising a couple of aspiring writers be-

hind bars. He also was attempting to save a third prisoner from execution. Tully's personal life, however, was starting to fray. Bouts of depression, "moods," beset him and his three-year marriage to 24-year-old socialite, Marna Myers Tully, was beginning to unravel. Despite their troubles, he dedicated *Shanty Irish* to Marna.

In the foreword to a later book, *Blood on the Moon* (1931), Tully described *Shanty Irish*.

In "Shanty Irish" was depicted the background of a road-kid who became articulate. Down the avenue of years my grandfather, who dominates the book, has been very real to me. I can still hear, on quiet nights, the whisky rattling down his bony throat. That he talked a great deal was natural, of course, being Irish. He was a sad old man with a broken dream in his head and a fear of death in his heart.

Broken dreams fill *Shanty Irish* but Jim inherited neither his grandfather's sadness nor his fear. In an early chapter of *Shanty Irish*, Jim wrote of his father. "A most amazing Irishman was my father—one devoid of sentimentality. A man without tears, he often seemed without pity." Like his father, Jim too was a man without tears. What made him different from both his father and grandfather—and from lesser writers—was his great capacity for empathy.

Mencken was the first to recognize the book's excellence and contributed a blurb which appeared opposite the title page.

If Tully were a Russian, read in translation, all the Professors would be hymning him. He has all of Gorky's capacity for making vivid the miseries of poor and helpless men, and in addition he has a humor that no Russian could conceivably have. In "Shanty Irish," it seems to me, he has gone far beyond any of his work of the past. The book is not only brilliantly realistic; it also has fine poetic quality.

Reviews of *Shanty Irish* were mixed. James M. Cain, writing in the *World,* praised *Shanty Irish.* Praise that Mencken believed, given Cain's "bilious" nature, would boost the book immensely. The *New York Post* concluded that *Shanty Irish* was " . . . Jim Tully's greatest contribution to literature. In our opinion it will become a definite part of our national belles lettres." The *New York World* review was so enthusiastic that the book's publisher, Albert & Charles Boni, included part of it on the book's dust jacket: "A yarn that soars up into the vaulted blue. It is, we submit, literature. In it, for a moment, the national letters have a glorious reversion to the roaring vigor of yore." The *Chicago Daily Tribune* was both amused and shocked, citing the book's "blasphemy" and "words that aren't pretty" but was forced to conclude that "there is something sturdy and lusty about it." Perhaps not quite so lusty as Tully intended. In the one-legged stranger's story, Tully originally had the old man saying, " . . . gigantic copulations shook the sky." Tully would later complain bitterly to Maxwell Perkins about Boni's poor job of editing *Shanty Irish*. Whether out of timidity, as Tully suspected, or sloppiness, "copulations" became "osculations" in the printed book. A review that must have particularly pleased the author washed up from Dublin. The *Irish Times* concluded that *Shanty Irish* was "far in advance of anything he has previously done." It praised the book's "clear-cut economy of phrase and stark precision of characterisation, a book wherein tragedy is splashed with humour and comedy steeped in sadness . . ." Even Upton Sinclair, with whom Tully had been feuding, wrote that *Shanty Irish* is a "chunk of real life. It made me feel human and humble, which is good for anybody."

Not everyone approved. The leftist writer and founder of *The New Masses,* Michael Gold, who had praised Tully's earlier work, panned *Shanty Irish,* blaming the pernicious influence of H. L. Mencken. And another Dublin paper, the *Irish Independent,* under the heading, "A Slobbering Idiot," considered Hughie as just another drunken Irishman. And in Tully's hometown of St. Marys, Ohio, his cousin Gertrude Lawler wrote that the book was widely read, but never openly discussed.

Shanty Irish sold well in both the United States and England, and as late as 1945, Tully wrote Mencken that the book was still selling. The book's success certainly had much to do with the comic and roguish old Hughie, whom Jim tried making the main character in a stage version of the book, *God Loves the Irish.* It was never produced, but Hughie would make a return appearance as a principal character in *Blood on the Moon.* What made Hughie and *Shanty Irish* different was that Tully was the first to treat the Irish-American experience in something other than strictly comic tones.

In *The Columbia History of the American Novel* (1991), Emory Elliott concluded, "that by its focus on a poor Irish family [*Shanty Irish*] set the theme and by its title's ugly epithet set the tone for the breakthrough of Irish-Americans into the fiction of cultural mediation."

"I developed early a capacity for remembered sorrow," Tully wrote in *Shanty Irish*. "It is possible that I remembered too much." It is from this well of remembered sorrow—and empathy—that Jim Tully fills *Shanty Irish*.

CHAPTER I

THE GREAT FAMINE

My grandfather was known as old Hughie Tully. Born with the gift of words, he was never without a tale to tell.

Drama was as natural to him as corn to an Ohio farmer. Arson, treason, and sudden death were as common in his Irish boyhood as gossip about the King of England.

He respected nothing among men. He was capable of turning death into an Irish wake and pouring liquor down the throat of the corpse.

Still a child, I was with him and my father in a saloon.

"You must have had a lot of fun in Ireland when you were a kid," I said to him.

Grandfather looked at me. and then at his glass.

"There was niver any fun in Ireland, me lad— It was always a wailin' and a weepin' country. Hearts full of the great sadness and stomicks empty of food—fools prayin' to God, and starvin' on their knays.

"Ireland at its bist was a hard country—we lived wit' the pigs an' the geese—we petted thim an' thin we ate thim—

"All who saw not alike were bayten—an' stabbed an' shot an' strangled."

The bartender wore a beer-spotted apron. He poured more whisky, and gave me a glass of beer. He started away with the whisky. I could hear the gunshot rattling in the bottle.

"Lave it here, Pat," said my grandfather, "it is better so, me son—Jim will pay you for the whole bottle." No sooner was it placed on the wet table than grandfather poured another drink.

He looked at my father.

"Did ye iver think, Jim, why me and you ain't dead?" He gave a few heavy sardonic chuckles. My parent made no answer.

"I'll tell ye why—we're like me father—only a bolt o' lightnin' from God Almighty's merciful rainbag can kill us."

He pushed his empty glass away.

"Me and your mother lived through the Great Famine—a-suckin' the wind and drinkin' the rain on the bogs.

"There was niver nothin' like the famine of '46—an' the boy here talks about a lot o' fun.

"What a bunch of liars an' brigands we Irish are. We'd cut the Pope's throat for a nickel an' burn 'im in hell for a dime. There was only the one trouble with the Great Famine—it didn't starve enough of thim. An' thim that lived through it didn't live. They died an' come to life agin. An' yere niver the same once ye rise from the dead—somethin' has gone out ov the heart o' ye. No one saw Jaysus after he rose. He hurried away in a cloud—the soul ov Him torn an' bloody at the side ov his Blissed Father.

"The dear Irish niver see the truth—an' the greatest fighters in the world—they git licked iv'ry time they start.

"Though I hate to say it—bein' a devout Catholic meself—an' believin' in the Holy Womb of Mary—but they should aither kill

[3]

all their praists or put 'em to work—it would be the same thing, be God."

"Tell me about the Great Famine," I asked eagerly.

"Be quiet, me lad, and don't talk out ov your turn—'tis a bad habit."

He shook his head violently.

"I think I swallowed some gunshot—I'll explode in a minute—

"An' wasn't it in '46 that a Catholic Baishop said how the pizzants bravely paid their rint—the good craytures, he called thim—the lazy holy bum." His face wrinkled. "And didn't old Danny O'Connell tell 'em they were the finest pizzants on earth—the poor fools an' they belaved it—min who talk without thinkin' are the bane ov Ireland—their tongues mane no more than broken church bells callin' 'em to prayer.

"An' Danny O'Connell's son said he thanked his just God that he lived among payple who would rather die ov the hunger than cheat the landlords of their rint—" He muttered with contempt—"The damn fool."

[4]

"An' Mike Davitt—the son ov pizzants from the County Mayo—who knew my payple —it was him that rose in his wrath and asked why in the hell he wasn't kicked into the River ov Liffey.

"Ireland couldn't even fight thim—the eyes ov the pizzants were glazed over with the great hunger. Death coughed on all the roads.

"I was a young man in '46 when the potatie crop failed. You see, Ireland is aisy to grow grass in—and the cattle git fat—an' they bring more money than pizzants, as they should— they eat and don't pray—and they don't bother their wise heads about what they don't understand.

"It was the year ov the Great Stupor—and the fife played to the tunes of death in ivery house.

"Whole families would sit on the fence and look at the ground where no potaties grew—

"An' England made min to build roads with the starvin' death above thim. They felt they'd pauperize Ireland, so they said if they give 'em somethin' without labor—

[5]

"An' the pizzants left on ivery ship. Two hundred in the steerage from Sligo to Liverpool—and half ov thim tramped to death—hundreds and hundreds of thousands were put out of their huts because they could not pay the rint. The poor divils, wit' cracks in their brains an' water for blood.

"An' durin' all this time a lot o' the dear blissid Irish earned the money to pay their way to America in the coffin ships, by pullin' down the homes o' their brither pizzants after they'd been excited in the road because they couldn't pay the rint."

The old man sighed—

"Windy wit' brither love are the Irish—as are all people who belave in lies, but in their hearts they're traitors—one with another—they'd sill the soul of Charlie Parnell himself—which they did—for an early potatie. Him that talks about brither love is a fool— He don't know the Irish."

A kindlier look came into his eyes.

"An' maybe I'm wrong an' too severe—some o' thim were sad when Parnell died—he was

the first an' the last an' the whitest gintleman
Ireland iver had—he was too good fur thim.
The pizzants were not his payple—he was an
aigle fightin' for sparrows. An' whin they had
the great aigle down an' his wings were tied an'
the manure of the barnyard was in his eyes—
thin what did a dumb sparrow of a pizzant do
but call Kitty O'Shea a whore—an' what did
Parnell iver do but break a law to git a woman
he loved—and Gawd—I'd love a woman like
Kitty O'Shea meself—I would, I would—but
that is no matter now."

He drummed the table with his labor-
twisted fingers.

"It is of the famine I'm talkin' whin the
dumb Irish wint starvin' to glory, wit' the
praists showin' thim how to die like Christians
gnawin' at the wood of the cross."

He rubbed the left side of his breast—

"It's the damned rheumatiz eatin' at the sad
heart o' me— It'll be me own bad luck to die
before John Crasby—an' thin he'll brag about
dhrinkin' Old Hughie Tully into his grave—
but that's no matter ayther."

[7]

He took his hand from his heart—

"But this ye kin remimber, me lad—niver to forgit— There niver was a plot in Ireland that didn't have its traitor. Two Irish—an' one tells on the other.

"Blind min lookin' at truth are the Irish—wit' shamrocks an' lies where their brains ought to be."

He pulled his glass toward him and poured another drink. My father sat, silent as an owl on a limb at mid-day.

I watched my grandfather eagerly.

"An' while the great famine wint on England took from Ireland two million pigs an' sheep an' cattle—

"There was no food to eat so the pizzants ate grass and seaweed and potaties that were rotted— A million ov the poor divils died with the achin' pain in their guts—a prayin' to Jaysus who loved the poor—

"They died like whipped curs a-whinin' under the lash—whimperin' from the ditches and the bogs.

" 'Holy Mary—Mither of God—pray for

[8]

us starvin' sinners now an' at the hour of our horrible death—Amen,' they prayed.

"Fifty million dollars worth of grub went out of Ireland—an' the poor bedraggled bastards watched it go—an' starved—

"But ye couldn't make thim think—they belaved in God." The whisky rattled down his heavy throat.

"Be careful, Dad," said my father, "the boy here—"

"Shut up—he's got a brain in his head—he's his old granddad's boy, an' it's best he hears the truth.

"They wandered along the roads lookin' for grub. They pulled green turnips from the fields. They ate dead horses that died ov disease—an' mules an' dogs—aye—an' a woman ate the dead limb of her only child. The dead were found with grass in their mouths—aven in me own county of Mayo—they ate nettles and wild mustard that stuck in their guts like glue."

Old Hughie's face went heavy with indignant pain.

"Irishmen left the God damned country like it was a mangy dog and not the purtiest land in a purty world.

"Thousands an' thousands—maybe a million left in a year—an' thank God I was among 'em."

His voice lifted.

"We left on ships that were shaped like coffins—and so they were—for many—

"We were huddled in the dirt an' the sickness—with no light an' little air—women an' men an' childred all fightin' away the black death together.

"One can niver hate all the Irish afther seein' 'em die—thim that are crossed wit' the Danes die snarlin' like the tigers they are.

"Many were so sick they couldn't move—they sat or laid wit' their mouths droolin' green slobber an' their faces twisted like apes wit' nails in their ears.

"All over the ship were the moans— 'Blissed God have mercy—have mercy, Blissed God— Take me away wit' ye—take me away—oh—

oh—oh—oh—Dare Savior of all poor sinners —take me to the grave away—'

"Their cheeks pushed their jaws in—an' their skin turned green—an' their eyes wint blind—an' many died in the madness—poundin' their heads on the floor."

The old man gulped twice.

"There wasn't enough canvas to wrap them in whin they died—so it was aisier for the sharks who didn't have to tear it off."

The old man poured more liquor with a firm hand and looked at me. "An' I aven thought yere own father would die—me boy," he looked defiant for a second. "It's damned bad cess he didn't, I guess—but I was younger thin —an' I wanted him to live."

My father did not look up. He sat, hunched over, finger and thumb clenched to his glass. The ends of his long mustache nearly touched the table. Impassive as fate, he was more inarticulate than my grandfather. He was not so forceful a man. Old Hughie has ever remained the strongest oak in the blighted forest of the Tullys.

[11]

He hit the table—

"Ay—an' I didn't tell ye me lad—they buried so many payple they wasn't coffins enough to go 'round—so they put a hinged bottom on the coffin—and they dropped it in the ground with the body as nice as you plaze— an' the poor divil laid there with his hands folded like he was glad to be dead—an' they lifted the coffin from about him an' used it for a hundred more min that had starved—an' soon they threw the dirt in his Irish face foriver." A short silence followed. "Suffer did they all—but no good did it do. It only made ashes out ov their bones."

The old man shook his head as if trying to rouse himself from a haunting dream. He rose. We followed him out of the saloon.

"Tell Him," he said to his son, "ye'll be goin' away in the mornin'."

"Yes," replied my father, with unconcern, "Back to Van Wert County—to throw more mud with a crooked stick—"

"Aw well—'tis better than havin' the rheumatiz near yere heart—an' a man like John

Crasby braggin' that he put ye in yere grave."

"Wait a minute," suggested my father.

He went into the saloon again and returned with two quarts of whisky. He handed my grandfather a bottle, the old man placed it in a side pocket.

"What are ye to do about the boy here?" Old Hughie asked my father.

"He'll be goin' to work in the mornin'—in a restaurant—washin' dishes."

"It's not a job for a Tully," grandfather exclaimed—"but aw—'tis no business o' mine." Then stopping suddenly he said to my father: "I'll see ye later." And to me—

"Good night, me boy."

CHAPTER II

THE DAY OF HEROES

OLD Hughie Tully was considered an educated man among the Irish peasants of his period. He could read and write.

My great-grandfather was not so fortunate. England did not allow Irish Catholics to attend school in his youth.

He lived and died in ignorance abysmal.

Five feet high, and nearly half of that across the shoulders, his neck was a mass of muscle and according to my grandfather, "Like steel ropes, be God."

Reared in a hut on a rain-washed bog, he cursed England and Cromwell, and lifted heavy weights for drinks.

He lived to be nearly one hundred years old. He was finally struck by lightning.

"It took an act of God in his mercy to kill him," was Grandfather's comment. "No man could do it, begorra. He could knock a horse down—an' choke a bear to death. He hit a man with his little finger one time and it bashed in his skull. He hit a Protestant in Cork an' it broke a preacher's nose in Dublin. . . . He was a man he *was*—he *was*."

Old Hughie Tully's well of memory was filled with drama.

Two months later we again sat in the rear of Coffee's saloon.

My father had money in plenty. He had finished the ditching contract.

Dressed roughly, the men faced each other.

"How's the dirt in Van Wert County, Jim?"

"Heavy—like glue—it stuck to the shovels and the scrapers—a hell of a job."

"Oh, it takes yere old dad to show ye how to throw the dirt. When I first give up the piddlin' and took to the shovel I could throw a barrel o' dirt over a house—I could—I could. . . ."

"Take another drink, Father, an' ye can throw it over the moon—a house is not a bit high."

"Ye will have yere joke an' doubt the word

[15]

o' yere old father—but there's only one man
who could ever throw the bog to kape even with
me—an' he was—an' he was Timothy Walsh
of long dead mimory— God rist his hot soul."

My grandfather gulped his red liquor and
looked at me with threatening eyes.

Fearful of so strong a gaze I looked at my
empty beer glass.

My father called the bartender. Grandfather continued talking.

"He was a murderer—he was, he was. He
killed the meanest man in Ireland—and the fattest. He was the boss ov a hundred men and he
made 'em dig like worms. They cursed him an'
he bate thim an' he sneered, 'Go on an' curse, ye
scum o' the earth. See the big belly o' me, and
the big chest—indade ye rascals I'm growin'
fatter on yere curses— Glory be to the Blissed
Savior.'

" 'Indade an' ye are,' says Timothy Walsh,
'God bliss ye,' comin' up closer to him in the
bog, 'how would ye like to go to heavin—where
all the rich belong?'

" 'I'll go to heavin in me own good time,'

[16]

says he, 'an' it's not the likes o' ye who'll have divil a word to say about it.'

"'All right,' says Timothy, says he, 'but say yere prayers now— I'm not the one to send ye to yere God—wit' the poison ov yere soul in yere heart— God 'ud think ye were a snake an' condemn ye to crawl over the hills of England foriver.'

"'Ho, ho, ho,' says the boss, 'it's not to be that ye'd be killin' me—kill one o' yere own dirt if ye must have the gore o' men on yere hands. . . .'

"'It's not the gore o' min I'd be after,' says Timothy, 'it's the gore o' divils—with a dead piece o' bog for a heart.'

"Over the bog was comin' the boss's son.

"'Ye better hurry if ye want to see a good man die,' says Timothy, and with that he give a run an' a jump—an' a dagger a foot long went into the heart o' the meanest an' the fattest man in Ireland.

"He crumbled up like a sack o' blood with a hole in it—an' it poured all red and turned thick on the bog. An' whin the son came close

[17]

he saw Timothy with the dagger—long an' bloody.

"'An' I'll kill ye, too,' says he, 'with yere thievin' dead father an' ye to take his place. God Almighty damn the soul o' ye! That ye kin ride in yere fine carriage—an' run over me while I dig in the bog that ye don't starve. . . .' He ran toward the stalwart young son—an' the madness was upon him—and the son ran like the English before the Irish at the battle of Fontenoy—an' Timothy was after him with his father's blood shinin' red on the dagger. . . . 'Run as far as ye like,' says he, 'but I'll catch ye at last . . . an' sind ye to yere father now so lonesome and dead. . . .'

"An' they ran by the cottage o' Mary O'Brien. She was ould and she couldn't see well—an' she walked on a crutch—an' she heard a man stumble an' fall over in her yeard. An' a man screamed, 'O God! O God! O God! Don't murder me!' Then she heard blood gurgle an' the dagger go up an' down. Then she heard the dead man become quiet—

an' look up at the sky with his dead eyes. Thin Timothy kicked the dead jaws o' him—until his boot rattled agin' 'em like stones.

" 'Join yer father, ye braggin' bastard,' says he, 'an' tell him I sint ye—with yere damned heart empty o' blood that ye sucked from the poor.'

"An' Mary O'Brien hid in her house tremblin' like a frozen dog."

The bartender poured more red liquor in my grandfather's glass. I watched his laughter-wrinkled face go stern.

"Tim Walsh came to me father's house. 'Shake hands wit' a murderer,' says he to the ould man. An' me father says, 'Who did ye murder,' says he, an' Tim says, 'Who could I be murderin'? Why, the Blakes—father an' son. . . .'

" 'It's too bad,' says me father, 'ye should o' killed his three brothers. . . .'

" 'Give me time,' says Tim Walsh.

" 'Does any one know ye did it?' asks me father.

" 'Nobody but God—an' he always winks

[19]

whin a landlord dies—ye kin aven hear the angils snickerin' in heaven. . . .' "

My grandfather lifted his glass and clicked it against that of my father's.

"Here's to ye," he snapped, "an' to the forever gone an' weather-beaten and lonely soul o' Timothy Walsh."

The old man's voice crooned soft as dawn on an Irish meadow.

"Tim was only twenty-eight, with a head like a lion's and shoulders as broad as me father's an' a heart that was bigger than all Ireland whin it's rainin'. . . .

" 'Stay here with me,' says me father.

" 'No—it's to America I'll be goin' with me bloody hands an' me soul unafraid. . . .'

"Well, they got Timothy . . . an' came the day of his trial.

" 'Bring in the witness to identify him,' says the judge.

"In came Mary O'Brien.

"They stood Timothy among the men—an' gave her the long rod to lay upon the man's head she had seen with the dagger.

"Ye niver saw a ghost look so terrible. She was bent double, an' she had no teeth, an' her hands were bones. She smoked an ould pipe an' she snarled. Maybe she wouldn't know him who had rid the earth o' the monsters.

"An' they gave her the rod . . . an' all looked quiet as the dead on Ash Wednesday.

"She picked up the rod an' leveled it around the room. My father screamed, 'My God, Mary. . . . Betray not our kind. . . .' His words were took up by others, an' they roared. . . .

" 'Betray not. . . . Betray *not*— Betray *not* our kind.' They made of it a song until the constable made the room be still.

"Ye could o' heard a feather drop. Mary O'Brien looked in ivery face . . . an' thin like the old witch that she was—she laid the rod on the head of Timothy Walsh—an' the judge said: 'Him shall we hang.'

"In the ould days in Ireland ye wint to the rope sittin' on yere coffin in a cart. Ye got there an' ye met Canty, the Hangman . . .

an' they said that he couldn't sleep at night for the spirits o' the min with the strangled necks kept tryin' to choke him.

"Timothy was ordered to be hung near the spot where he'd killed ould Blake, an' there were many thousands of people gathered there —for they all loved Timothy.

"The horse died— O' poison maybe—on the way to the gallows where Timothy sat a-laughin' on his coffin.

"He took the medal ov the Blissed Virgin from around his neck an' gave it to me father. . . . 'Wear it,' says he, 'till I be avenged.'

" 'That I will,' says my father, 'till the blood runs like water from the hills. . . .'

"An' they could git no other horse to drag the cart. For if ye have a horse to drag a man to death in Ireland, 'tis niver forgiven ye—ye belong to the *Informers*.

"They wanted Tim to help carry his coffin.

" 'Indade an' I'll not carry a bed I don't want to sleep in . . .' an' four men carried the coffin—an' Timothy walked behind it.

"Tim's neck was bigger than a bull's. Big

bunches of muscle thicker than ropes strung it to his head.

"He walked along the road, with his coffin goin' ahead, the beloved Irish payple cursin', cheerin' an' laughin' at him o' the brave heart that was about to die.

" 'We'll see ye in Heaven,' yelled Mary O'Brien's nephew, him o' the black heart.

" 'Ho, ho,' says Timothy, 'not if ye go there, ye dog. . . . I'll leave on the wings o' the angel Gabriel—rather even in Hell with Cromwell than with ye in Heaven.'

"The coffin must have been heavy, for the men changed hands—an' one was tired. . . .

" 'Come,' says a constable to me father, 'an' give a hand on Timothy's coffin.'

" 'Indade,' says father, 'I'll carry the coffin ov no friend before he's dead—not if ye bury me in it. . . .'

"It begun to rain, an' the drops rattled on the coffin like lost wet souls.

" 'Hey, hey, hey,' says Timothy to me father, 'the God in his heavin is givin' the worms a drink.'

[23]

"He dropped his big chin on his breast an' walked like a man in a trance. The raindrops rattled louder . . . an' Timothy begin to laugh. A man o' ice an' iron he was—wit' a streak of fire between.

"An' they says to him at the foot o' the gallows, 'Will ye have a holy father confessor, Timothy? . . .'

"And he looked with flames o' scorn in his eyes.

" 'Indade an' it's niver a praist I'll—if ye bring him that is nayther man nor woman to me, ye'll have to hang me agin for murder—which would be a bother to the Holy Mither Church. . . .'

"An' they put the coffin down as careful as glass.

" 'Ah, ha, ye bosy,' says Timothy, 'don't break me glass bed . . . for I must see me way through Hell in that.'

"An' the crowd came in closer an' closer . . . an' Timothy walked up the gallows . . . the muscles in his neck bulgin' like hunks o' steel.

[24]

"Canty, the Hangman, stood—his fingers itchin' on the rope. 'Have ye anything to say, before maytin' yere God,' says he to Timothy.

" 'Was there iver a time an Irishman had nothin' to say,' says Timothy, 'give me a dagger—ye murderer for England—an' I'll say it in yere heart.

" 'Gather round me ye slaves o' England, an' an unjust God, ye poltroons—rise in yere might with daggers in yere hands an' cut the throats of yere masters. . . .'

"The constables rushed around at him at the words.

" 'Kape yere hands off o' me—I want to go to Heaven clane. . . .' Timothy looked as happy as a praist at his own wedding.

" 'Put the rope around me neck with no traitor's hand upon me—an' I ask ye me friends when ye take me away—to let none o' thim to cut me from the rope.' (For the rilitives an' the friends took the body in thim days.)

"They stood Timothy on a cart an' fastened

[25]

the rope around his neck. Then a dozen o' the lowest men in Ireland pulled the cart from under him.

"He threw his neck back. His body went straight like an iron rod—an' he snapped the rope—an' he fell to the ground—an' thin me father an' a thousand others rushed in. There was sich a battle. Ye could hear the heads crackin' as far away as London . . . an' they took Timothy with the rope draggin' from his neck . . . an' they kicked the coffin to splinters.

" 'Git him agin—over our dead bodies,' says they, an' me father stood like a block o' stone a-knockin' traitors across the Shannon River twenty-eight miles away . . . ye could hear their heads hittin' agin' the trees on the other shore . . . an' they popped like empty paper sacks. . . .

"An' they rushes to the cottage o' Mary O'Brien . . . an' there was no one at home but a black cat.

"They shut the doors an' stood with clubs at the windows.

[26]

" 'Burn the house,' yells they, 'for the cat is Mary O'Brien!'

"An' the flames crackled up and spit an' spit—till soon there was ashes and the bones o' the cat.

"An' as they hurried over the hills to hide Timothy, he laughed in me father's ear, an' he says, 'That damned rope scorched me neck,' says he."

* * * * * * *

My grandfather hit the table with his glass. My father looked as one who had heard the tale before.

"It's licker I want," said the rugged ex-peddler, "Jim—yere father's glass is empty."

The bartender filled the glasses.

My grandfather gave me a knowing look.

"There was min in Ireland in thim days, me lad—better min niver lived—like dogs," says he.

The glass went toward his mouth with the speed of a bullet. He threw his massive head backward.

"I'd never heard ye say that Granddad was

[27]

at the burnin' of the car," observed my father.

"The hell he wasn't," the old man retorted sharply, "he'd have burned the Pope that mornin'." He motioned for the bartender again.

"Ye see—they *was mad*."

My father laughed.

With eyes of wonder I look at both.

"What became of Timothy Walsh?" I asked.

"Ah—that's the sad thing—that's why he's been dead to me so many years . . . indade it was fine the bolt of lightnin' hit me blissed father before he knew it.

"Ye see—there was some Scotch in him, an' he didn't know it. But they smuggled him here to America, an' he became converted—an' inded up a Prisbyterian minister."

The old man looked at his empty glass dolefully.

"A man with a neck like that."

CHAPTER III

A BED OF PANSIES

So poverty-stricken were my mother's parents that three children remained in Ireland long after the others had come to America.

My mother was a house servant at fifty cents a week before she was twelve years old. Within a year she obtained work with another family at one dollar a week.

My grandmother started a boarding house when my mother, Biddy Lawler, was fourteen. Mother and daughter took care of fifty laborers, cooked three meals a day, made the beds, cared for several small children, and did the washing besides.

In two years they saved fifteen hundred dollars. With this money my grandmother purchased what is still known as the Lawler farm.

Then Biddy Lawler married my father. She moved with him into a log shack in the woods. There they remained three years.

Sick with the ague, the mumps, yellow jaundice, and malaria fever, they emerged poorer than on their wedding day.

A woman of imagination, my mother had all the moods of April. Married at sixteen, she was dead at thirty-two.

The mother of eight children in as many years, she had an unconscious sense of drama, and no humor. But even humor would not have saved her. She was one of those sad women who lived by ignorance and died by faith.

Her hair was auburn, beautiful, and very long. She wore it in heavy braids which reached to her knees. Her eyes were large, deep brown, and tragically sad.

Her mouth was puckered always in a childish pout. The lower portion of her face was too strong for the current conception of beauty.

Her younger sister, Moll, had dark hair and dark flashing eyes. She was wistful and stubborn.

They had attempted to join a Protestant church. All the other Lawlers gesticulated wildly over the episode. My mother received the news in rigid silence.

Her pink flesh turned white. I was with her in the yard when my father told of the event. She held my hand till it ached.

Only once, and not until months later did she ever make comment.

The following Christmas, her relatives, a dozen in all, drove over the snow in a bob-sled to spend the day with her.

Moll accompanied them.

With an unyielding sense of Irish drama my mother walked to the sled.

She called them all by name, beginning with her father and mother—saying in turn:

"Father, you can get out— Mother, you can get out—Tom, you can get out—" and so on until she came to Aunt Moll—

"But, Moll—*you* can't get out. You can never darken my door."

She turned defiant, and walked into the house, the long auburn braids of her hair swinging like censors aflame.

A brother followed and pleaded with her.

[31]

He might as well have talked to a stone on a grave.

He pleaded forgiveness on account of Christ's Birthday—it would make her children happy—

With mouth set tight, she shook her head.

"You may never see her again," the brother said.

"I *never* will!" Her mouth went tight again.

My uncle returned to the sled.

He took his seat near Aunt Moll. She was not much over twenty years old. An Irish colleen type, her features were regular and beautiful. Her eyes were vivid blue.

Many writers describe the Irish as loquacious in anger or war.

Greater mistake was never made.

These twelve, with the wounded pride, sat silent, and stared down the snowy road.

The horses started. The bob-sled glided over the road. All were gone.

My mother talked no more that day.

Early the following spring my mother was

bearing another child. She had a cow to milk, the housework to do, a husband, a father and six children to look after.

She found time to make a bed of pansies and surround them with violets. She watched them tenderly.

A late frost came and shriveled their many colored heads even with the stems.

She cried over them as though they were dead children.

CHAPTER IV

A MAN WITHOUT TEARS

A wife, six children, two cows, one hog, a blind mare and a sense of sad humor, were my father's possessions.

We lived in a log house, in and out the windows of which the crows of trouble flew.

My father was a gorilla-built man. His arms were long and crooked. The ends of a carrot-shaped mustache touched his shoulder blades. It gave his mouth an appearance of ferocity not in the heart. Squat, agile, and muscular, he weighed nearly one hundred and ninety pounds. His shoulders were early stooped, as from carrying the inherited burdens of a thousand dead Irish peasants.

A man of some imagination, he loved the tingle of warm liquor in his blood. He was for fifty years a ditch digger.

The house, built by himself, contained four

rooms. In it six children and their parents lived.

Relatives visited us for days at a time. I early learned to sleep like a contortionist.

We reached our home by a muddy or dusty lane according to the Ohio season. It was in the center of a dense wood a half mile from the main road.

A deep ditch ran in front of the house. It had been dug by my father.

The section in which we lived was known as the Black Swamp. It was flat for many miles.

The artificial St. Marys Reservoir, ten miles long and seven wide, was not far away. It drained the muddy water of many counties and spawned a pestilence of mosquitoes.

A soggy muddy basin, it was an ideal section for a ditch digger. My father had all the poverty, children and work he could manage.

My father came from Ireland with his mother when a lad of ten. My grandfather had preceded them three years before. After seven weeks on the ocean, he was five days reaching Ohio from New York, a distance of eight hundred miles.

At heart my father was an agnostic without knowing it. His wife relied much on God. He did not interfere.

Aware of the trap in which life had caught him, he bowed to his peasant futility like a gentleman.

He treated his children like unavoidable evils, and deserted them early.

Violating all rules of health, he was never ill.

He would read by the hour. Whether it helped him mentally, I know not. With but one exception, he was a man who never made comment.

He was nearsighted. When reading, he never moved his eyes. A country newspaper, a frayed volume of Shakespeare, or a medical almanac, it moved backward and forward within two inches of his left eye.

He would give his last dollar away—and take another man's last dollar without compunction. He gave his money to the person nearest him at the time.

He was always in debt.

He was a man whom calamity followed.

Once, while ditching in a nearby field, he saw his house ablaze. The family was away.

He ran across the meadow and rushed up the stairs.

He saved a corn husk mattress. He jumped with it out of the window.

My mother arrived with neighbors soon after. She hastily took a small gilt clock from the mantel. It was all she had of beauty.

A farmer threw a large crock of eggs into the yard in order to save them.

Two cows and Blind Nell were in a small enclosure adjoining the house. The cattle broke through the rails and escaped. Blind Nell remained.

She was the delight and wonder of our childhood. A five-acre woods was her summer home.

Totally blind, she could walk through it without touching shrub or tree.

She would enter the forest by the same route and come out at the same place each time.

With tail ablaze, she now stood whimpering, still.

My father seized a revolver.   I followed him.   He crashed a bullet through her skull.

She went to her front knees, as if in prayer for the dying.   Her hide was bare as a glove. She twitched once—and was still.

A most amazing Irishman was my father— one devoid of sentimentality.   A man without tears, he often seemed one without pity.

He patted the forehead of the dead mare, while his house burned to the ground.

Much was said against him.   He was called a child deserter, a whore-monger, and a drunkard.

A product of people too much given to the vice of slander, he never made an unkind comment on others.

*　　*　　*　　*　　*　　*　　*

After the fire we lived in an old schoolhouse for two weeks.

[38]

My father borrowed five dollars. A few neighbors helped us.

Farmers and relatives gathered later to help build our new home. They brought cast-off pieces of furniture for our use.

They felled trees and hewed them. Oxen dragged them from the woods.

Straight trees of smaller size were cut and fitted as rafters. The home was completed by night.

Then mother brought her flock home, and life went on as wretchedly as before.

Father had the oxen drag Blind Nell to a spot in the woods.

She was never buried.

Black buzzards circled the sky above her.

I pointed toward them.

My father could not see that far.

I told my mother about the buzzards.

She planted a seed in my childish mind that day. While baking cookies she kindled my imagination with a strange tale. It has grown with the years.

* * * * * * *

The buzzards had once been beautiful eagles. Their homes were on the high mountains. Once a year they accompanied a fairy train to the moon.

In the long ago when returning from the moon they had seen a slender man with a sad face. He carried a heavy cross on his shoulders. His eyes had the look of one who gazed down a road in eternity.

He knelt, with head down, under the weight of the cross. Rising, he stumbled once, and fell. He looked upward imploringly at the green and blue eagles.

Three little sparrows came out of the sky and looked in pity at the sad man with the cross. They called aloud to the far-off eagles to come and help him.

Immediately the sparrows were turned to golden-throated nightingales. Their voices filled the world with music. The eagles flew higher and higher, laughing at a man who carried a cross on a rough road to a little hill which overlooked a never-to-be-forgotten valley.

Out of a jagged hole in the sky came a giant's head. His eyes were bigger than the sun. Worlds could be seen burning in them.

He lifted an ocean in his hollow palm, and pressed it to his forehead to cool the heat from his eyes.

"I must speak without malice," he thundered, "and punish without vengeance."

The eagles hung in the air, like iron birds attached to invisible wires.

The giant scooped all the snow from the mountains of the world and held it over his heart.

"My heart must be cool—for my punishment is severe."

The eagles trembled before him, their wings outspread.

"I am the King of the Thunder," the giant said in a low whisper which shook the sky, "and I saw you refuse help to a child of the stars in the land of human Buzzards—who eat the hearts and souls of the loveliest and the purest birds we are forced to send among them. And so for this offense—you will become as

one of them—forever and forever and forever."

As the giant said the three *forevers* the earth
opened.

He smiled at a fleece of cloud that trailed
across his right eye.

"The man you refused to help has come
back to us—with what earthly buzzards call a
thief on each side of Him. They were cruci-
fied for taking that which they owned as much
as the rest of their fellow buzzards."

The giant sighed and wiped a tear from his
left eye. The ocean with which he had mopped
his forehead rolled downward.

"Too bad," he smiled, "that may cause a
deluge in the land of buzzards. Oh, well, if
a million or two are drowned we can always
hatch others out of the eggs of rattlesnakes."

The eagles laughed.

"Silence!" thundered the King of Thunder.
"Why do fools laugh at the misery of men they
do not understand?"

He wiped his other eye . . . Another ocean
fell to the earth.

[42]

"Too bad—too bad," he sighed again—
"Every time the earth cracks down there a
great man dies—It has cracked twice now in
ten million years. One was a carpenter—and
the other an unknown fool."

He looked sternly at the myriads of eagles
before him.

"Get ye down to the earth—and as buzzards
remain—flying always in circles like the minds
of all the other buzzards down there."

The Eagles' feathers went black. They flew
earthward, their eyes on the alert for carrion.

The sky closed.

The Giant was gone.

CHAPTER V

CHILDHOOD

I EARLY learned, with my brothers, the tricks of the woods. We knew how to go with the wind when tracking rabbits. We used the moss on the trees as a compass, claiming that it was always on the north side of the tree.

We once robbed a quail's nest and placed the eggs under a setting hen. Two of the eggs hatched in a few days.

The hen, feeling that her task was done, rose from the nest.

No larger than hickory nuts, the two quail followed the hen about the place.

They were a constant grief to mother. Several times she gave us ten cents each to lose them in the woods. We were careful to see that they found their way back to the barnyard. In a few days, mother would give us ten cents again. The large red hen would cluck at her two nervous children in utter dismay.

At last they went to the woods, and returned no more.

When my clothes were fit to wear I went to mass on Sunday with my ragamuffin brothers and sisters. The church was situated in Glynwood, an Irish village, five miles from St. Marys. Across the road was a cemetery where rustic wanderers, far from Ireland, were buried. Children, early exhibiting an Irish contempt for death, played tag upon the graves.

Three saloons were close to the church. My father often dallied too long at the bar. He often reached his seat in church without reverence in his heart.

Shoes were scarce in my childhood. From early spring until late fall I wore them only on Sunday, when I called at the house of God.

Barefooted, I ran in the early morning frost to bring the cows from their straw shed in the woods. I would warm my feet where they had lain all night.

The roads in our section were merely wagon tracks through woods and fields. Often, when father drove his oxen to town, I would go along.

My bare feet would hang from the wagon and trail in the muddy water.

My father seldom talked to me. There was a restful kindness in his silence. His personality, save on a few dramatic occasions, was negative. My mother's was positive. They lived together peacefully for sixteen years.

The county paid a bounty of one cent each for dead sparrows. I was too young to kill, but my older brothers each owned a sling shot and rifle. I accompanied them to the county commissioner, who lived eight miles from our home.

Down the road we went with our hundred dead strung across the neck of the Blind Nell.

As though in mourning for the occasion, the horse walked slowly. As she could not be made to move faster, my brothers jumped off her back and ran ahead.

When we reached the commissioner's house, I rode into the lane like a freckled king delivering a dead feather-ruffled army.

The commissioner counted the birds as a miser would pennies. He loomed large to me.

His beard was heavy. There were two red

spots on his face which it did not cover.

A great many pigeons hopped about his barn-yard.

He gave us a silver dollar and scolded us for killing the birds.

Years later I heard that he had been in love with my mother.

She did not want to marry "out of the church."

We would often wander through the woods and tap the sugar maple trees.

Our mother had a reason for the sweetness of the water:

It was a very hot day in August. Three fairies wandering from Ireland sought rest under the shade of many trees. All would draw in their leaves at the approach of the fairies.

Worn in body and foot sore, they came at last to a small tree. It had been beaten sideways by the wind. Its leaves became larger than ele-phants' ears when it saw them approach. They rested under its shade a long, long time. When all was ready for the journey back to Ireland, a heavy wind roared over the meadows and through the woods. It bent the little tree until its branches touched the ground.

The fairies could hear the tree's heart aching. One branch said to the other, "If we break now we will never be able to give shade to such sweet tired little people again."

The other branch said . . . "Oh, we cannot break—not for ourselves, for that doesn't matter—but suppose we were all wrinkled and dead and some one needed shade on a hot day like this—these little people are so woebegone that we must fight to keep alive for their sake—and the sake of others."

The fairies heard the words. For, according to my mother, it is the gift of no other fairies in the world but Irish fairies—to hear pine trees whisper to birds in the mountains—to hear eagles talk to tigers in the sky. The head fairy said to the others: "I want to be alone for just a little moment."

He waved at a passing cloud. Out of it stepped a beautiful young lady dressed in blue. Her blue eyes danced like the sun on Easter morning. Her skin was whiter even than mother's. Red roses were in her cheeks. Her dark hair was studded with golden stars. She wore a large cloak with vivid red lining. She stepped down and talked to the head fairy.

He motioned to the bent little tree. The other fairies heard the beautiful lady say, "How lovely—such a good deed should never die— and just think—those branches thought not of themselves at all—at all." The three fairies and the beautiful lady looked long and admiringly at the little tree. The beautiful lady threw a kiss to each branch.

Suddenly the tree grew many feet. It became the most shapely tree in Auglaize County. Birds came from all the directions of heaven and sang within its branches. There were orioles green and gold, and eagles—red, purple and blue. The eagles sang like canaries, until many scarlet birds came and took up the song. Then the beautiful lady whispered:

"Give the tree and all its sisters eternal life, and make their blood sweet and warm, and their roots to go deep down into the earth so that no

[49]

wind only out of the hand of Almighty God can ever make it bow."

A mighty roar was heard in the woods. It was all the other trees complaining.

"We intended to give shade," they said.

And the beautiful lady called back to them, her voice softer than dew under the feet of the child Jesus:

"I shall not judge you . . . but these little travelers could not find rest under the shade of your intentions. It was a happy chance that I happened to be coming by this way. I have so many worlds in which to see that the flowers grow properly that I have not been over this section in a million years."

She paused, the roses glowing in her cheeks.

"But I shall carry your good intentions to our Heavenly Father—and he will judge you kindly."

She turned to the little fairies:

"Would you like to ride to Ireland with me?" she asked.

"Yes, indeed, most beautiful lady," they replied.

[50]

A cloud swooped out of the sky. It was more graceful than an eagle on a windy morning.

"We shall be in Ireland in thirty-two minutes," said the beautiful Lady.

They waved at the friendly and now beautiful sugar maple tree, and were lost to sight in a second.

*   *   *   *   *   *   *

We took our dog Monk everywhere with us. Always the vanguard of adventure, plumed tail ever wagging in joy, his eyes were ever sad.

The priest gave him to my mother when he was a puppy six weeks old. I learned to walk by holding to his side.

A thoroughbred collie, he carried himself among Irish peasants as if they were his equals. He associated with no other dogs.

One day Monk ventured too near a rattlesnake. It struck him on the shoulder with enough force to knock him backward. He ran yelping away. Forgetting the snake in our anxiety for the dog, we followed him to the bank of a large ditch which ran in front of the house and circled back through the woods.

[51]

Monk hurriedly buried himself in the mud until only his head was exposed.

All our coaxing would not make him move. My father told us that it was a dog's way of curing itself of poison. It would require four or five days.

Patiently we waited. Each night before going to sleep I would think of Monk, alone, out in the mud.

We carried meat and water to him every day. He would touch nothing, and growl his disapproval if we came too near.

He finally came home with a starved appearance and a limp in his shoulder.

The Prodigal Son was not treated with greater kindness.

A culvert six miles away was often our destination. Its roof was a "cattle guard" made out of steel spikes to keep cattle from wandering on the railroad tracks.

We could tell time by the position of the sun. We knew just when the train passed the crossing. We were literally tattered sun dials.

We awaited the approaching train in the culvert with Monk. It vibrated over the ground a half mile away and bore down upon us with a terrible roar.

One day we decided to tease Monk. We crawled into the culvert without him. Monk tried to follow. We would not let him in.

The train roaded toward the culvert.

Monk, baffled, ran barking up and down the tracks. We yelled . . . "Get away! Monk! Get *away!* Get *away!*"

But Monk, feeling that we were in danger, dashed along the rails.

We scampered from the culvert. The whirling dust made it impossible to see or talk for a short time.

At last we regained our voices.

"Monk—Monk!" we yelled.

We could not see him.

"Monk, Monk! Come Monk—come Monk! Nice Monk—come on—we was only teasin'! Come on, Monk!"

Tom, my older brother patted his knees and snapped his fingers.

[53]

We scanned the tall grasses on each side of the track.

At last Tom said: "Maybe he got mad and run on home—dogs do that."

To console me, he added: "That's jist about what he did—we'll find him right in the summer kitchen with mother."

Tom fell on the ground a short distance further.

"Monk — Monk — Monk! Please look, please, please. We didn't mean it Monk, *please*, PLEASE."

Monk's eyes were partly open. His legs were bent under him. His body still quivered. He tried to open his eyes. They went shut.

We placed him in an easier position.

He moaned; and moved no more.

We laid him upon a board. Murderers could have felt no worse.

A freight train passed, on its way to St. Marys. I can still see the engineer, red kerchief about his neck, waving, these thirty years.

"Will we tell Mother and Virginia how it happened?"

Tom, my nine year old brother, replied slowly—"Yes—"

A farmer, hauling gravel from the Forty Acre Pond stopped his team.

He was a shriveled, weather beaten man with a face the color of burnt brick. He put his hand on my shoulder.

"Lost your dog eh—oh well—don't you cry —you kin git another one—there's lots o' dogs."

He helped us place Monk in the wagon.

As it stopped in front of the house mother and sister Virginia came to the road.

Monk's mouth was grim in death. His front paws were crossed. They cried over the thoroughbred martyr for the peasant Irish. Red-eyed with weeping, mother looked at me.

"What will you do?" she asked.

Tom said, "Mother."

Holding both her hands to her ears, she said: "I know, I *know*."

Monk's name was never mentioned to mother again.

We buried him in a far corner of the woods.

[55]

Three hard maple trees formed a triangle over his grave.

We built a fire upon it, and chanted all we could remember of the Litany for the Dead.

CHAPTER VI

A BRAND SNATCHED FROM THE BURNING

GRANDAD Lawler was the father of as passionate, unyielding and stubborn a group of men as ever turned over the ground for grub. More like robber barons than peasants, four of his five sons were as unrestrained as eagles.

They were all devout Catholics during mass on Sundays. Roisterers, drunkards, braggarts, picturesque men and poor farmers, they made of their parents' lives a long tornado.

If not mad, they were at least not completely sane.

They were physically brave. Their tempers were impetuous; their intelligence always superior to their environment. Open to every impression, they were extremely volatile. They lacked perseverance. They resented discipline. Boastful and quarrelsome, they were excessively vain.

Their simplicity was often childlike. Their

[57]

feelings were always austere and intense. They were violently active and lazy by turns. Their interests were as narrow as those of savages. They followed the four seasons without the pain of wonder. If a neighbor died, he went to heaven, hell or purgatory. His destination was not debated among them. They feared death —more as a cessation of violent living—than as an eternal quietus.

They often wept over trifles, and were adamant over events that would have wrecked less primitive men. They could veer suddenly from tears to the crashing laughter of barbarians.

No man among my mother's brothers was less than six feet tall, and none weighed less than two hundred pounds. Well built, well muscled—they were neither gaunt nor fat. No Lawler ever died slowly. Each man went— sudden as a pistol shot.

There was in all of them, a holdover from ancient days—a deep mystical strain.

They believed in ghosts, in fairies and in witches. In their hearts, ready to germinate at any moment, were the wild seeds of fanaticism and bigotry.

My mother was baptized Maria Bridget Lawler. It was shortened to Biddy. Maria, we were told as children, was the name of the mother of Jesus. St. Bridget was said to have been the foster mother of Christ. My mother was proud of the name.

Her father first came to America from Ireland in 1850. It was said of him that he was "as good a man as ever lived." His wife, ever a bitter woman, the apple of whose life had early turned sour at the core, followed him a few years later.

Only once did he ever do anything in anger. That was when his daughter Moll Lawler had astonished the countryside by attempting to join the Walnut Grove Methodist Church.

She had been working as a "hired girl" in the home of a farmer six miles away. Her brother Dennis, driving through the neighborhood, told the family that Moll was nightly at the Mourners' Bench.

The Lawlers were seated at the supper table.

"It's a Methodist she'd be," Dennis said to his father.

"A Mithodist—niver—" my grandfather thundered. "I'll skin her alive first—rather indade were she in her grave." He crashed his fist on the table. A heavy plate rattled to the floor.

"Hitch the bay mare up Dennis—we'll save the soul ov Mollie."

Dennis hurried to the stable. In a short time the horse and buggy awaited grandfather.

The old man stood on the porch for a minute and watched the night creep down the road. His lips shook.

"All right, father," yelled Dennis. Grandfather climbed into the buggy beside his son.

Neither of them spoke for over a mile. The bay mare trotted swiftly. Dennis said at last, "Even the mare's in a hurry."

"She's a good horse," returned my grandfather grimly, "more sense than Moll, she has." He scraped his heavy boot on the dashboard. "What in the whole world puzzest the girl?" he asked suddenly.

[60]

"Maybe the devil," replied Dennis, "they say he likes to steal the souls of good lookin' girls."

"Well it's not Moll's that he'll steal this night . . . I'll bash in his skull before he does."

The lights of the church could be seen in the distance.

It was full of country folk in whose hollow souls echoed the myths of Salvation. They called on the Lord for strength to rise washed and dripping in His precious blood.

They screamed, knelt, expostulated, and rolled on the floor.

The preacher was a man with fanatic eyes sunk deep in his head. He lived on a farm and preached at two country churches.

A heavy black mustache hid his mouth. He wore a long tailed coat and leather boots. His energy was dynamic, his voice deep and vibrant. In a section of the world where all men were religious fanatics, he gave other creeds no quarter and asked none himself. He called the Catholic religion rottener than hell.

His name was anathema in Irish homes.

The Lawlers, always headstrong, fanatic and opinionated, could never forgive a man as bitter as themselves.

He walked up and down in front of the Mourners' Bench, his arms frantically waving. He removed his long coat and threw it across the large Bible. A woman rose from the Mourners' Bench, perspiration dripping, bonnet hanging down her back, hair falling over her face. She clapped her hands together and screamed, "Only Jesus can satisfy me!"

"That's right, Sister—only Jesus can satisfy you—"

He droned the words.

"Only Jesus can satisfy me . . .

"Only Jesus can satisfy me . . .

"Glory to God, sister—you are right—only Jesus can satisfy the women of the world."

She kissed the minister fervently.

They all gathered about my Aunt Moll who knelt at the Mourners' Bench, body swaying back and forth. Her dark hair touched the

[62]

floor. The minister placed both hands on her head. The young girl sobbed convulsively.

The minister sobbed with her. Then his heavy voice boomed the first line of a song.

"There were ninety and nine that safely lay—"

It was taken up by the entire congregation.

"In the shelter of the fold,
But one was out on the hills away,
Far off from the gates of gold,
Away on the mountains wild and bare,
Away from the tender Shepherd's care."

The next verse was filled with the thunder of hysteria. Male voices, cracked, powerful and weak, sang the words:

"Lord thou hast here thy ninety and nine;
Are they not enough for Thee?"
But the Shepherd made answer, "One of mine
Has wandered away from me;
And although the road be rough and steep
I go to the desert to find my sheep."

[63]

The song reached even greater heights:

"But none of the ransomed ever knew
How deep were the waters crossed,
Nor how dark was the night that the Lord
passed through
Ere he found his sheep that was lost.
Out in the desert he heard its cry,
Sick and helpless and ready to die."

The voices became lower, more plaintive
. . . pleading . . . questioning. For kneeling before them was one from a hated church.

"Lord, whence are those blood-drops all the
way,
That mark out the mountain-track?
They were shed for one who had gone astray
Ere the Shepherd could bring her back.
Lord, whence are thy hands so rent and torn?
They are pierced to-night by many a thorn."

The voices raised.

"But all through the mountains thunder-riven,
And up from the rocky steep,

There rose a cry to the gate of heaven,
    'Rejoice! I have found my sheep!'
And the angels echoed around the throne
    'Rejoice, for the Lord brings back his own!' "

The preacher wiped his forehead.

"Ah, Brothers and Sisters—we are the shepherds of the long lost sheep brought back from the vale of ignorance and superstition. Beautiful and contrite in the sight of the Lord—long wandering in the meadows of hated Rome. Hands rent and torn from saving a lamb from the hideous mouth of hell."

"Amen! Amen!" the congregation shouted, "Hallelujah, Thine the Glory—Hallelujah! Amen!"

The preacher continued:

"Ah—twice more glorious in the sight of God to bring back one who is perishing away from the true light. We should be shepherds of the blind multitude who stumble on paths far from the seat of God, the most beloved. Torn by the briers of hate, our sister here is yet to know the saving grace of our Savior . . ."

[65]

Suddenly an old farmer jumped up and down.

"Another sinner bound for glory," shouted the minister, as the farmer sang—

"Blessed Lord I'm glad I'm free—
No more of the devil's chains for me—
Glory to God in the Highest—"

He fell to his knees, shaking in a frenzy of rustic delirium.

"Let us hear more of the Lord's power, Brothers and Sisters," shouted the minister.

A heavy red-faced woman jumped up. By her side sat a little farmer in overalls.

"I thank God that my husband here is now a laborer in the Vineyard of the Lord. He saw the light after thirty years of blindness. All his bad habits dropped from him.

"Goin' home he took it out an' I pleaded wit' him an' he fought wit' me."

"Amen Sister—Amen," from many voices.

"He took it out again an' I pleaded wit' him —an' at last he threw the whole terbaccer plug into the ditch."

"Glory to God," the minister shouted.

"Stand up Brother Ed—so all can see the great victor over evil."

Bashfully the farmer rose.

"Give us the testimony, Brother," loudly suggested the preacher—"Tell us of the sheep long lost in the wilderness who saw the light at last—"

The farmer tried to sit down. His wife pushed him upward. The congregation joined the preacher in asking his testimony.

"Well, I'll tell you Brothers an' other folks 'sembled here under the Lord's roof that we fixed last year. I ain't much on speech makin' but I wanta say—that my heart ain't been so light in nigh on thirty year.

"I worked in the vineyard when I was a boy over in Lucas County—but then I got married an' back slid as it were—an' I took to chewin' terbaccer an' drinkin' a glass o' beer when I drove to town wit' a load o' corn—an' went from worse to worser until I became so low I'd sit an' play cards in the saloon. My wife here prayed all that time—or them years,

I mean—she musta got to thinkin' I'd never come back to the fole—then when our pet cow died—I give in—an' Brothers and Sister-folk —here I am glory-be." He made an ineffectual attempt at feigning joy.

"Amen," was shouted often.

His wife rose again.

An old man stood quickly and talked faster.

"Brothers and Sisters, the Lord cured me of paralysez when two big doctors from Lima failed—"

"Praise be his Holy name—cured of paralysez—think of it Sisters—two big doctors failed —praise be the power of the healing Lord," the minister clapped his hands.

The farmer's wife still stood. She started to talk.

Another voice from a young woman drowned her words—

"Blessed be the Lord's name—he took the measles away from my baby, and chicken pox away from me in a week."

"Blessed be His name," from the preacher, leaning over my aunt again.

[68]

Many hands clapped.
A voice started:

One more river—
And that there river is Jordan—
One more river —
There's one more river to cross—"

"There is no more rivers to cross for our new found brother in the Savior," shouted the preacher, "He is washed in the blood, my friends—washed in the blood—"

The rustic chanted—

"I am washed in the blood of the Lamb, Lamb,
Lamb—
I am washed in the blood of the Lamb—"

The preacher and other religious farmers hugged Moll in the delirium of salvation. They shouted, "Holy God—Let us pray—"
They dragged each other about. Rustics in the rear of the church flirted and laughed.
Suddenly, so strong is suggestion to vacant minds, they too would hear a divine voice and

[69]

go forward to the Mourners' Bench. There
they remained kneeling, often night after night.
Then exalted by bovine madness, they acknowl-
edged their Savior and their God.

My grandfather and his son entered.

Moll, their Catholic pride and joy, was being
caressed in the name of religion by a group of
fanatic farmers.

Amid hysterical and convulsive sobbing and
groaning, the preacher began to sing,

"At the cross, at the cross,
Where I first saw the light,
And the burden of my heart rolled away—
It was there by faith
I received my sight
And now I am happy all the day."

A lull followed.

My uncle shouted a parodied line of the verse
just sung—

"And now I am in the family way."

All arose from the Mourners' Bench, and
turned to the door.

There stood my grandfather and my uncle,

the former calm, the latter defiant. They towered above all the other men in the church. They walked to the Mourners' Bench.

Methodists and those about to become such made way for the strong apostles of the Pope.

Their heavy boots could be heard pounding on the pine floor.

Dennis Lawler grabbed his sister. He held her, screaming, tight. He put a heavy hand over her mouth.

My grandfather faced the fanatic audience—

"Ye ignirint Methidist devils—it's me own lamb ye want—to nibble at lies with yere brayin' goats—an' divilish well ye prove that if he throw yere seed on the ground with enough madness it'll take root—The nerve of all of ye Protestint bastards, to lay yere dirthy hands on a daughter of mine! Indade I'd sooner see her rottin' in her grave than to become one o' ye. A lot of Mithidist spalpeen ye are—Stay in yere own hog pens and go to hell in yere own way without draggin' her that is mine. Agin I say ye durthy bastards—"

The preacher rushed forward. My grand-

[71]

father's heavy hand laid against his devout jaw. He rolled near the pulpit.

The religious fanatics gathered in anger about the two apostles.

"Take Moll," my uncle commanded, "and follow me."

Never did devotion charge more viciously.

Methodists fell to right and left, nursing bruised jaws. Women scratched at my uncle. He pushed them among the seats.

My grandfather followed with his burden. Moll's recent brothers and sisters at the Mourners' Bench tried to snatch her from his arms. They tore her clothing from her.

At last they reached the buggy and drove away.

"Ah, Denny," laughed my grandfather, "it's proud of ye I am this night—for ivery time ye stuck out yere fist a Mithidist fell down."

CHAPTER VII

A MAN WHO STOLE HORSES

My mother's oldest brother began life a horse thief—and died a banker under an assumed name in Canada. He ruined his parents and served thirteen years in the Ohio penitentiary.

At seventeen he came to America from Ireland, to join his parents. He brought his younger brother and sister with him.

John Lawler was tall, reticent, with an aquiline face and a hot temper. In mentality, the greatest of the tribe, he was ruthless, relentless, and domineering.

He watched his brother and sister lowered into the sea—dead from fever.

On reaching Ohio his mother asked for her other children.

"They died on the way over," he said.

His mother's face went gray with horror. She closed her eyes for a moment, opened them suddenly and closed them again. She clasped

[73]

and unclasped her hands. Staring as if in a trance, she screeched at her son:

"Did ye save no medals—no trinkets—nothing?"

"No."

He worked on a farm until he was twenty-two.

A girl whom he had with child sued him for three hundred dollars.

He induced his mother to pay the amount.

Under pretense of future matrimony, he borrowed the money from the girl, and went to Illinois. He remained three years.

After he had defrauded the girl out of the money, his mother had, in the manner of an Irish virago, put a curse upon him.

"Aw—an' ye traitor—to drag your ould mother's good name in the dirt—God'll forgive ye this—Indade an' indade an' may the divil make a rubber ball outta your soul to bounce aginst the gates o' hell for all eternity . . .

"An' may it bounce in an' outta the flames, agitin' scorched a little at a time foriver an' foriver . . .

"An' may the ghosts of all the men who've betrayed women hant ye till the day ye die—an' may they throw rocks on your coffin—a-kapin' ye awake and smotherin' inside . . ."

But this was only an outburst. When anger was not upon her she remained loyal.

John Lawler developed a mania for well harnessed young horses and new wagons.

When the girl in Ohio was safely married to another yokel, he stole a team and wagon and returned to his parents.

He sold the outfit in Ohio, and reëntered Illinois with a team stolen near home.

A country maiden in Illinois became with child by him. Undoubtedly embarrassed, he went back to Ohio and confined his operations to that State.

He sold the team and wagon with which he arrived and bought two decrepit horses and an old wagon. He drove eighty miles to a large new barn which stood a half mile from a house.

He put the old team and wagon in the barn, and drove away with a young team and a new wagon. He burned the barn.

[75]

Charred remains of horses and wagon were found among the ashes. In time it was apparently forgotten.

He went to his parents' home and remained two years. He had undoubtedly given up his penchant for other men's horses. He worked steadily on his father's farm with the team.

A silent fellow, and working always alone, he had left few traces of himself.

One morning two strange men called at the Lawler home. My grandmother received them cordially. They wanted to visit her son, John. He would not be home until late that day.

The men had dinner with my grandmother and waited. She talked long of her eldest son. When he drove the handsome team into the barnyard, he was arrested.

He was tried, convicted, and sentenced to fifteen years in the Ohio Penitentiary.

The team which he had stolen wore no shoes. The horses, which he had burned alive, were well shod. This oversight made him a convict for thirteen years.

* * * * * * *

Grandad Lawler was unusual among the Irish. He forgave everything. He was the first to relent toward his Methodist-chasing daughter.

He had, like my mother, a phobia—love of God.

His wife had long since left him. He lived at our house.

His sensibilities were not those of the horse thief offspring, with whose fate his mind was corroded.

An immense Irishman, with blue pockets of pain under his eyes, he would sit in a chair and rock back and forth an hour at a time.

Rubbing the gray beard that had once been fiery red, he would say—

"I'm the father of John Lawler, I am, I am —and may God have mercy on his soul—and *mine!*"

And mother would say to him—

"Never mind, father—God has a purpose in all this."

He would break in with,

[77]

"Yes, yes Biddy—I know, I know—may God forgive me—I didn't mane it."

Another blow awaited him.

His second son, Dennis, was a drunkard.

Of softer material than his brother John, he too, was hard.

He deserted the old man when needed most.

"And have ye heard from Denny?" he would ask my mother.

"No, father—but I'm sure he will—Denny was never a hand to write much."

Grandfather rocked in his chair, while mother stood in the doorway, her apron to her eyes, crying.

I could not get the full significance of the parting at the time.

I can still see the old man rocking fiercely, and my mother crying, as the form of a young, heavy-shouldered red-headed man faded down the road.

His dog followed him a short distance then returned to the house.

My mother's hair fell in long coils over her breasts. As Uncle Dennis turned on the main road, she dropped her apron, sobbing convulsively, clutched the braids of hair tightly as if they were ropes upon which she was swinging.

She walked to the road, and returned to the house.

They never heard of Dennis Lawler again.

The Lawler farm was lost in the battle of Irish sentimentality with justice.

After their son's journey to the penitentiary the proud old man and his virago wife went down the muddy road, penniless—in another man's buggy.

They left the farm in the hands of a rich German landowner and separated later over my grandmother's temper and the conduct of their son.

My uncle, Tom Lawler, married the German's daughter. His children inherited the land.

It is still the Lawler farm.

CHAPTER VIII

THE COLUMBUS PENITENTIARY

My uncle rode to the prison with a fat Irish deputy sheriff. He had taken prisoners to Columbus for twenty-one years.

They traveled half the distance without talking. His arm fastened to a seat by a handcuff, the sardonic horse thief looked out of the window at the dreary Ohio scenery.

"Fifteen years ain't long," said the deputy— "a lot of men get life." The horse thief looked at him—and nearly smiled. "You'll get usta it after a while—MAYBE—"

A man with neither remorse nor pity, Lawler looked out of the window again.

Two other prisoners came aboard at a county seat. The guards chatted. The train stopped. Passengers rushed to the depot dining room.

"You'd better eat a lot—it'll be your last chance for fifteen years," reminded the guard with a touch of malice.

He ate in silence, his leg chained to the leg of the table.

By noon Lawler was in prison garb. There had come over him blank dismay.

A brigand at heart, he had an eagle's pride. He entered the prison, silently defiant. He remained the same during thirteen years. Prisoners around him were in endless turmoil with the guards.

He practiced no wiles to gain favor. Whether it was aloof poise or a silence that bred respect I know not. But in thirteen years no unkind word was said to him.

The deputy warden called him the first day.

"Go your own way," he said to him, "Hold your head high and tend to your own business. There's no horses here and no women—you'll have a chance to go straight—and remember keep everything to yourself. You'll be safe then. For if two men know a thing in here—I'll know it—I know everything any two men in here know—don't trust anybody but God—and don't pray out loud."

Lawler stood with intense silence before him.

[81]

His manner must have worried the deputy warden—

"Tell me," he said quickly, "how you came to be a thief."

Lawler made no answer.

The deputy handed him a book of rules and a card. "Read them good," he advised, "every time the card's taken away it'll mean you stay here that much longer."

Lawler nodded his head.

The deputy handed him a sheet of paper, a pencil, an envelope and stamp. "You can write a letter now to whoever you want to—and one each month. The State'll furnish the envelope and stamp." Lawler handed the writing material back and shook his head, "No."

"Don't want to write?" asked the deputy.

Lawler answered tersely—"No."

For a month he was lonely and unbroken.

The deputy warden talked to him at the end of ten days.

"It'll come easier," he said, "soon you can get a banjo and a boy and settle down for a while."

The years drilled deep into his consciousness.

He learned that a prison was also run by politics. He learned the wisdom of the deputy warden. News traveled as if on invisible wings. Everything seemed written on faces for all to read.

He was in charge of the "condemned cells" during the last two years of his imprisonment. He carried food and solace to men about to die. He often found notes in the cells of the men who had gone.

One man was hung a week before another who had turned state's evidence.

"I'm damn glad to go," he wrote, "I can hear the white buzzards of death flyin' around my cell now. I'll get started ahead of —— and wait along some dark road of hell and cut his throat as he passes by."

* * * * * * *

No one met John Lawler when he came from the penitentiary. He arrived in St. Marys at night—alone.

My mother as usual, had been silent and sad.

[83]

She walked between me and sister Virginia in the woods until sundown.

Slowly, a few feet apart, we approached the house.

The sun was a caldron of many colors. Above it were dark clouds. An owl hooted and made me afraid. Woman and girl caressed me, saying no word.

Six miles away, the lights of St. Marys made a white splotch in the night.

We walked into the yard. My father sat, in mud spattered overalls, near the kerosene lamp.

The light shone through the window on the face of my mother. Her brown eyes were heavy with tears. The newspaper rattled in my father's hands.

Mother stepped backward as she reached the door.

My sister urged her.

"In just a minute." she said. "You get supper, dear."

Virginia went into the house.

Mother took me by the hand and walked toward the road. She looked intently toward St. Marys.

A man came out of the dusk. Mother held my hand.

The man drew nearer, greeted my mother, and passed on.

The echo of our neighbor's feet could be heard on the lonely road.

Late that night John Lawler came to the house. Three of his brothers were with him.

Heavy bodied, they talked in low tones.

He finally said: "They may want me in Illinois. If they get me—they'll get me dead— I'm not safe here . . ."

The arrival from prison was silent as doom.

"This is Virginia," my mother said, "she was born afterward." John Lawler nodded his head. "The three others were born *afterward* too—"

The ex-convict looked at my father whom he had always liked. For Jim Tully had never passed judgment upon him.

"And how are you Jim?"

"Fine John—are ye going to stay among us —there's a home here—"

"No Jim—thanks," was the answer—"it's away I'm goin' before the morning sun!"

Bottles of liquor were on the kitchen table.

The five men drank.

"Gawd Almighty," the ex-convict jerked the words—

"What a hell of a price—what a God damn hell of a price—I'll burn in Hell forever before they get me agin—"

"John—John—" muttered my mother.

"Biddy—be kind," urged my father.

"Yes Biddy—you and all—it's the mud of Ohio I'm shakin' from my feet forever— and never again will I look a horse in the face."

He jerked one of the bottles from the table. The whisky gurgled down his throat like water.

"God in Heaven, John," implored my mother. He looked at her, the quart bottle in his left hand, nearly empty.

His magnificent body trembled as if fire had shot it through.   A rough bravado came to him.

"Biddy," he ripped out, "it's thirteen years I was in Hell for horses that are dead and the hunger of woman so great I'd have slept with a hag—"

He looked about him sternly—

"There's only one way to know a prison—Biddy—steal horses—God damn my black soul —what a fool I've been, eating my heart out till I wished to God the jail would burn—thirteen years—think of it—the same place at the table —the same grub—the same cell." He shuddered. "God Almighty."

A noise was heard outside.

His father and mother entered.

Long separated, they were not joined in the misery of their son's homecoming.

They advanced with hesitation. They looked at their eldest born as if he were from a strange land.

A gust of wind blew the door open. It made the lamp smoke.

There was scarcely a greeting.

"There is much I niver can say," mumbled the old man.

[87]

"And much that I daren't," added the old lady.

The ex-convict laughed bitterly. His teeth showed white and strong in the light.

"There's much I never want you to say—enough has been said and enough has been done—it was I that took the punishment—that had the mares of horrible night in my cell."

The horse thief's mother smiled forlornly.

"It was not alone were ye punished—we who niver stole horses suffered the nights and days with ye," she snapped.

"Maybe so," returned the son quickly, "but I was the one who went to the pen and stared at the night till my eyes burned hot in my empty head."

"And will ye," asked the mother, "take Aggie Regan with ye as yere wedded wife—she's been waitin' all these years."

The ex-convict laughed again.

"Indeed and I shall not—I'll pick up a woman when I get there." He gurgled another drink. "It won't be hard now that I'm out of jail."

The old lady looked at her son with scornful eyes.

An uncle peered out of the door.

"It will soon be light in the east," he said.

Several roosters crowed, one after another. The group listened. My grandmother passed within a few feet of my father. Both their faces were stern set.

They did not speak. It was through them that all the brood of trouble was in the room. But of that they were not aware.

"So ye won't take her with ye," my grandmother snapped, as if it had suddenly dawned upon her.

"May the Mither of God forgive me for bringin' into Ireland a child with nayther a heart nor a soul," she moaned.

"Mother—please," pleaded my mother. "John will soon be leaving us."

"Yes mother—soon will I be leaving—and forever and forever—that will be long enough —the damn sun can burn everything in Ohio— and no bucket of water would I pour on it." He looked at my mother—"except you Biddy—

[89]

yere too white an egg for a black nest—may your bed be made of roses in Heaven."

He turned and looked into the unyielding eyes of his mother, then walked toward her. Sons and husband assembled in a group about the old lady. The horse thief pushed them aside.

"Let me hug you mother—once for all and forever—there is much to forgive me mother —"

He held the flinty old woman in his arms.

"John—John—" she half moaned—"I forgive—I forgive—maybe it was you that suffered—maybe—" Her voice trailed. Her aged arms went around him. Her limbs bent at the knees. She crooned to herself: "God—God—God—the breakin' heart o' me."

Her old face went stern and hard again. Her limbs straightened. "I'll forgive ye John and swallow the hard words I've said even if they choke me—an' belaive me my son—who came first—may the sun niver shine on my grave if I don't mane it."

"I believe ye Mother—you and all—for all

[90]

has been done that ever can be done—I'll die of my own poison like a snake in the mud."

My father stood apart. My mother stepped close to her own aged mother.

The door opened. Another uncle entered.

He wore a mackintosh with a cape. Rain drops glistened upon it. My father offered him liquor. He accepted quickly. Finishing his glass, he sighed with satisfaction.

He took my father's arm and stepped into the corner. All eyes followed him.

"Say nothing to the women," was the uncle's advice.

John Lawler caught my father's expression.

"It's time I'm going—good-bye to ye father —mother—" his eyes half circled the room— "and you Biddy of the good heart—and—and all—and all."

"We'd better hurry," advised the uncle in the mackintosh, "it may rain harder—and we've got some muddy road to travel—I've got the curtains up—no one can see you."

"But no one would know him after all these years," declared my father.

[91]

"Not even God," said the ex-horse thief.

My grandmother sobbed . . . "That the Lawlers be brought to this—sneakin' out agin in the night."

Soon mother love conquered shame. "Oh—oh—oh," she moaned.

John Lawler and his brother in the mackintosh hurried toward the door. Biddy Lawler and her father followed them. "My peace be with you," murmured my grandfather.

The old man's dignity must have touched John Lawler. Saying, "Father—Father—what a good man you are," he put his arm about him. "Peace can never be with me father—so long as I remember you." The old man stood, with weather beaten hands trembling and wrinkled.

Seven months with child, my mother, with sudden vehemence rushed into her horse thief brother's arms. Her hair fell in heavy red waves on her shoulders. All were astonished.

The pet of the Lawler tribe had fainted.

My father dashed a glass of water in her face.

The horse thief knelt suddenly and kissed her tragic wet mouth.

"Another drink Jim—please—please—the hard heart of me must be harder made—not even a hangman—"

My father cut in with:

"Take this quart with you,—it's a twelve mile drive you have."

The horse thief jerked the cork from the bottle impatiently.

"Let's all drink," he sucked at the bottle feverishly and handed it to his brother in the mackintosh. It ended in my father's hands. One more swig and it was empty.

My grandfather helped my mother rise.

Rain slashed at the window viciously.

"It's far ye can go yet—they don't expect ye here till to-morrow," a voice said.

The horse thief patted the shoulders of his mother and sisters.

The rain swept into the house as the door opened.

"Good-bye all — good-bye — good-bye — good-bye—and Biddy." The horse thief's voice was near to going soft. He turned swiftly and bolted after his brother in the mackintosh.

The rays of the kerosene lamp turned the pouring rain into silver. For a second the figure of John Lawler could be seen moving swiftly in a lane of light.

The Lawlers stood in the doorway and watched the released jailbird climb into a buggy. A horse's hoofs were soon heard sloshing on the muddy road.

John Lawler sat, with liquor roaring in his head, and rain running down his hard face. The horse turned onto the St. Marys pike and hurried westward.

Neither man in the buggy spoke for several miles.

The rain ceased. The sun rose. A train stopped at a small station.

John Lawler had gone from Ohio forever.

* * * * * * *

His parents died within a month.

Grandmother Lawler, her defiant spirit unbroken to the last, went first.

My grandfather followed her within a week.

[94]

His heart stopped one morning as he lifted his fork at the breakfast table. Made methodical by sixty years of economic slavery, he laid the fork down before dying.

He sat alone, breakfast untasted, stiffening hands on the table, massive chin on his breast. Gnarled, defeated, dead.

He was buried in consecrated ground.

CHAPTER IX

WATER TO DRINK

And all things danced upon the morning of the day Christ was said to have risen. According to mother, it was the sun shining on the tears of angels that made the April rainbows of Ohio.

A week before she died I trudged down the road with her to watch the sun come up.

I had never seen her quite so cheerful. Her mood enraptured me.

She stopped along the road to gather some "Johnny-jump-ups." I scrambled to help her. Each carrying a bouquet of the little flowers, we went on down the road.

Her hair, the passion of my childhood, was never more lovely.

I would often hold a braid of hair in each of my hands as though they were lines. Mother would then "play horse" with me.

But this morning, she was too busy to play.

For mother and all her children must attend
mass on Easter Sunday.

As the sun came up, her spirits seemed to go
down.

She sobbed and held me close as though the
mystery were too great for her.

My mood changed with my mother's.

We did not talk on our return to the house.

Mother poured water in an empty jelly glass
and placed the flowers in it.

* * * * * * *

She died on a rainy April night.

She had been ill for several days.

The little baby, as if in a hurry to leave the
dreary Ohio country, died too.

My uncle Tom awoke me. The kerosene
lamp threw weird shadows over my attic bed.
The rain rattled on the roof.

My uncle tapped my shoulder and said, very
slowly,

"Jimmy—your mother's dead."

He held a large red kerchief in his hand.
A tempestuous, sentimental, bitter, kindly and

fanatic man, he stood above me now, silent as the moon.

Stunned for a moment, I held his heavy hand. He said again, as if to himself. . . "Yes —Biddy's dead."

I could hear footsteps down stairs.

My two brothers were awakened.

No other words were said between us. We put on our few rags and followed Uncle Tom.

Into my childish mind a terrible thought came. I had killed my mother. The doctor had forbidden her to have water. The day before she had lain in bed, her throat parched. No one brought water but me. My sister Virginia had begged me not to listen to mother if she pleaded for water.

"It will kill her," she said softly, "the doctor says so."

Mother had a passion for keeping young.

She had the fear of death and old age which belongs to all great lovers of life. She often said to me, "I'm not so old—I'm just your oldest sister, Biddy."

I sat on her bed while she petted me.

"You'll get your Biddy a drink, won't you, dear? The doctor is just mad at me—and I'm so thirsty. You can run to the pump quickly— no one will know—and I'll never tell."

I found a large dipper in the kitchen and ran to the pump. I brought it brimming full to her. I took the dipper to the kitchen. Mother crooned to me when I returned.

She never told on me.

She begged her God not to take her. She told him the ages of her children in the hope that He would allow her to stay.

She died in the early thirties. Her last contribution to life's eternal merry-go-round, lay dead beside her.

Many people were in the room of death. They made way for Biddy's children. I advanced slowly—and stopped.

She did not seem dead to me. The lights from the lamps turned her hair into gold. Her eyes were half open.

Little more than a baby, I can see every scene, every gesture, as if it were yesterday.

[99]

A rosary was twined around her hands. Her fingernails were still pink.

Virginia put her arms about me. I touched my mother.

There had never been much love between the relatives of my father and mother. Both were in the wrong. Death had waved a flag of truce. They mingled sadly now.

Grandfather Tully stood in one corner of the room, alone. I hurried toward him.

My father joined us. Neither man spoke for some time.

"It will go hard on the boy here," said my grandfather.

"Yes—" my father returned slowly.

"Too much for Biddy it was—her mither an' father goin' in a month—an' John Lawler comin' back—an' Dinnis leavin' the way he did." My grandfather talked as if to himself.

My father said, "Yes, as slowly as before.

Our destitution was worse than usual. My clothing was not fit, in the eyes of my relatives, to allow me to attend my mother's funeral.

I stood in the road and cried until the hearse had passed from view.

A terrible brooding came over the log house. I would escape from it each day and wander with Virginia over the countryside.

It was soon decided to send me to an orphanage. I cannot recall that period of imprisonment without a feeling of overwhelming sadness.

I read a great deal. I knew Fox's "Book of Martyrs." I was certain that Martin Luther had hanged himself to a bedpost, and that St. Patrick drove the snakes from Ireland.

The routine of the days was precisely the same.

We children built all plans of the future upon the words, "when I go away." Leaving the orphanage became a mania with each child.

Three of my uncles came to the orphanage once in six years. My father did not come near.

I became a burden to the institution the last year. Those in charge were tired of seeing me.

During the final months of my stay at the

place I was worried greatly for fear that I would be sent to that penitentiary for juveniles —the Reform School. Two dozen boys lived under this threat. Our crime was—remaining too long at a place which we hated. Those who did run away were captured and returned. Each morning in school, we sang lustily—

"My Country, 'tis of Thee—
Sweet Land of Liberty"

Never did criminal put in six more terrible years of torture. And often I felt that I too was a convict.

I had given my mother water to drink.

CHAPTER X

A WOMAN WITH A MUSTACHE

ONE Sunday I received word that I had friends to see me. I could hardly believe the news. It was the third time in six years.

I hurried to the reception room.

Virginia and my older brother awaited me.

Little more than children, it was the first time in their lives they had ever been ten miles from St. Marys.

They had the expressions of people who face unknown terrors.

We were too overwhelmed to talk for some time.

My sister cried a great deal. Her arms would tremble as she held me. The touch of woman was a new experience. Dazed, it seemed as if I had been born into a world of which I had never dreamed.

I wore the little suit in which I had received

Holy Communion a few weeks before. I had
to change to older clothes with which to face
the world. The trousers were gray and patched
at the knees. The blouse was faded and worn.
The hat, the first I had worn in six years, was
redder than my hair. But clothes did not
matter.

The emotion of leaving overshadowed everything else.

There were some children whom long years
of loneliness had taught me to love. They cried
as they saw me leave. I thought not of them
that day.

A letter was sent from the superintendent
of the orphanage to one of my uncles. It
threatened me with the Reform School. He
did not respond. His wife told Virginia.

She was earning a dollar and a half a week
as a servant girl.

My brother earned ten dollars a month on a
farm. Together they decided to come and get
me.

The Grand Central Station in Cincinnati
made me speechless with bewilderment. My

sister held me by the hand—the blind leading the blind.

It was an excursion train upon which the fare had been reduced.

A crowd of glassblowers had travelled from a town near St. Marys. We all boarded the same car. Neither brother nor sister had the money to pay my way.

The glassblowers solved the problem to everyone's advantage except my own. They placed me under the seat each time the conductor came through the car. To them it was a joyous pastime. To me it was a long misery. The rolling landscape fascinated me. I could not enjoy the view from the window.

The men were all drunk.

We reached St. Marys at midnight. My brother walked to the farm. I stayed with my sister.

The next morning she borrowed five dollars with which to take me to my father. He was said to be forty miles away.

Whether or not we would find our gypsy father was uncertain. We talked but little. I

[105]

looked at the St. Marys Reservoir as we rode toward Celina and thought I had never seen anything so magnificent.

An old man left us at Ohio City. He was to take another road to Chicago. His body was twisted. His teeth were nearly gone. He cackled more than he laughed. A Civil War veteran, he had visited a brother at the Soldiers' Home in Dayton. His eyes were red as blood.

We became warm under his twisted smile.

"You'll get along my boy. You'll find your father. And some day you'll be a big grown man."

I watched him board the waiting train.

He had given me an apple.

After the old man had gone, Virginia hugged me and cried.

Worn from varied adventures, I slept with my sister's arm about me.

She wakened me at Haviland, a small station on the Cincinnati Northern Railway. Opposite was a two story hotel built out of rough pine boards. A tall grain elevator was a few hundred feet away.

We went to the hotel.

An immense woman met us. She wore a Mother Hubbard red and white calico dress. A blue and white checked gingham apron was tied about her. Her eyes were little and black. Her skin was swarthy. Her hair was sparse, coal black, and plastered to her head, which was shaped like a canal boat. A long black mustache was on her upper lip.

Virginia asked if Mr. Tully, the ditcher was at the hotel.

The woman, impassive, rubbed her mustache.

"He's been gone three weeks," she said, almost defiantly, pointing eastward. "Said he was goin' to Grover Hill—I ain't heard of him since."

My sister tried to be cheerful.

"Is it far?" she asked.

"Ten miles."

"Can we hire a livery rig?"

"Yes—" was the answer, "I kin have my man take you over—three dollars—you kin find him over there—it's a big ditchin' job—they say."

[107]

Looking at us with more interest, "Is he your pa?"

"Yes—" Virginia answered.

The woman called her husband.

Heavy and morose, he took us to Grover Hill.

"So you're Jim Tully's gal—an' the young 'un—"

"My brother."

A laugh stopped half way in his throat.

"Gosh—diden' think Jim ever stayed long 'nough anywhere's to have any kids." He slapped the horse with the lines.

"Your ma livin'?"

"No—" Virginia answered slowly. "I'm takin' my brother to our father—he's been in an orphans' home."

"Huh—too bad."

Our father had gone from Grover Hill some days before. No one knew where.

It was late afternoon when we returned to Haviland.

Virginia paid the three dollars and took me by the hand. The woman's eyes followed us.

We walked across the road to the depot, and

seated ourselves on a curved wooden bench, empty of words and forlorn, we looked down the railroad track. Two tiny streaks of gray, it seemed to stretch into the far-off sky.

The telegraph instrument clicked loudly. A wagon rumbled by on its way to the grain elevator. A farmer boy dangled his feet from the rear as I had done so long before.

Hungry and silent, we looked at a map which was tacked to the wall. It advertised a resort in Michigan. By one of those pathetic twists of memory, the map is still vivid in my brain.

"Don't you wish you was rich, Jimmy—we could go there."

I nodded, "Yes."

Virginia, like my mother, was almost beautiful. Her eyes had the same tragic sadness— the eyes of a hurt animal which must be hurt again. Still in her teens, she played with a long braid of hair and smiled whimsically.

I sobbed.

She put a finger to her lips—"Shhhsh, they'll put us out."

[109]

A terrible loneliness enveloped me. I longed for the children of the orphanage.

The ticket window opened.

"No more trains to-day," said a voice. The window went down with a crash.

We looked at the map on the wall.

The woman entered. Her frozen indifference had melted.

"What you children goin' to do?" she asked.

I looked at Virginia. She did not answer for a moment.

"We don't know." The words came at last.

The woman twisted her blue and white checked apron into a rope in her hands.

"Well, supper's ready, I didn't know. I hate to broach into people's business that hain't mine."

She led us to the hotel, talking volubly.

"You'd a thunk the cat had your tongue—you mustn't be like that—how'll you ever get along in the world. I didn't know your ma was dead till my man told me. The Lord never sent me no babies—it hain't because I didn't want 'em." She caressed me. "You know I could

[110]

thresh your father—did he know you were comin'?"

"No—we wanted to surprise him," returned Virginia proudly.

The woman seated us at a large table covered with red oil cloth.

It was the first real meal since mother's death.

There was chicken and gravy and biscuit.

The woman took a delight in serving me.

"When folks don't eat I think they're mad," she said to me several times. "I believe in lots of good food."

No meal has ever been so memorable.

The woman and her husband started eating after we had about finished. My sister bashfully pleaded with them to eat. They would not listen until we were satisfied.

After the meal we were taken to the private "parlor."

The woman raised the curtains weakly. The dying day came into the room. It showed heavy red chairs and a red lounge upon which was a red quilt. "I guess I'm gypsy. I like lots o'

[111]

color," she said to Virginia, "it makes me feel warm."

"So do I," assented my sister.

The woman's nails were broken, her hands red and puffed. She twisted her apron again and chattered on, as if to relieve a pressure on her brain. "So you hain't seen your father in a long time." She looked kindly at me. "He's the strange man, he is—he works till his back's half broke—and then he gives it all to the saloons."

She picked up a pink sea shell. "Ain't it purty—put it against your ear and hear the ocean roar. I ain't never seen any water— except Blue Creek and one time Maumee River. Many's the night I've sit and listened to it. I've always wanted to see the ocean." She laid it down with care. "I got it in Van Wert at the Fair—your Pa went with us—but he never got to the Fair Grounds—he got so drunk—when I scolded him he said—'Oh it's ivery man his own poison and the divil take us all.'" She chuckled and twisted her apron until the ends of her fingers turned white. "He was here with me three months—and he never mentioned a child he had in the world. Ah— but Jim Tully is the funny one—there was never anything in his room but empty bottles— he'd give you the world when he had it—but he never had it long."

"He was always good to us children," Virginia said defensively.

"But he should keep his own together—you didn't ask to come into the world."

Virginia smiled. "No—I never would ask that—"

"Why how you talk," the woman's words came quickly.

The girl smiled again.

"I hope you don't mean it," declared the woman, "you're too young and purty for such thoughts."

I slept that night in the room my father had occupied.

I wondered if the years had changed him— if he would know me. I could hear the noise of frogs and crickets and a horse's hoofs on the road.

[113]

Gazing into the darkness, my mind limped over the six years at the orphanage.

A feeling of bitterness toward my father came over me. I thought of my brother Tom, and tried to brush it aside.

"Dad had his troubles," Tom used to say. "Besides—we've learned to read and write. And maybe we wouldn't of done that if he hadn't sent us to the orphanage."

CHAPTER XI

WE had an early breakfast. The woman packed a lunch for us.

She put us on the train bound for St. Marys.

My sister borrowed five dollars and sent it to her. The woman returned the money.

Virginia then sent her enough red calico to make a dress.

The best friend I found in St. Marys, with the exception of Virginia, was my grandfather Tully.

He looms larger as the years pass. I was driven from one relative to another too young to work and too inexperienced to beg. The old man made of me a companion.

"Your dad'll be here in two weeks. It's glad I'll be to see him. I ain't had a decent dhrink in a month," he said when I greeted him.

He had a home with his daughter. By some ingenuity he was always well supplied with liquor. He would shake his immense well-chiseled head, narrow his eyes, and bite two words often. . . "Kape dhrunk."

It was the pastime in the wretched town for yokels to tease old Hughie Tully. So long as they bought drinks for the reveller everything was all right. If drinks were not forthcoming he would wander to another saloon.

I spent hours with him at the different bars.

Still a child, I learned quickly to drink and to observe, and to remember.

I developed early a capacity for remembered sorrow. It is possible that I have remembered too much.

"I like ye me boy," the old man told me after the first week. He could not realize my great sense of freedom after the orphanage.

I was soon to know all the saloon ruffians in the town. A shrewd judge of my character, my grandfather told me something of each of them.

Outspoken and diplomatic, there was in him a quality which often pierced the heart of things.

He had at least one great quality—detachment. He did not live to please others.

"I'm jist plain Shanty Irish an' I'll go to hell when I die—so thire's no use to worry."

He had been fond of my mother. He had no illusions about my father.

A few days before his son came to town he said to me—"There's somethin' wrong with your dad—whin the Lord made him He forgot to take the shovel out of his brain—he's niver bin the man he mighta bin—but oh well—it wasn't yere mither's fault—she came to a sad ind—as wimmin do—."

He pulled me toward him with a touch of blunt affection.

"But take not to heart what I say,"—his voice lowered, "she married yere father—a brave woman and a sad. Ye are like yere mither, me boy—yere worth the whole damn kit an' caboodle of 'em." Wiping the beaded alcohol from his stubble of beard, "An' yere like me too—the quick timper yere mither had—an' the heavy heart. She worried too much—an' for what—for nary the good it did

[117]

her." He paused, "She's in the Glynwood graveyard now watchin' the frozen worms crawl in the winter time, and lookin' at the roots of daisies in the spring." He rubbed the bottom of the whisky glass over the wet bar. "To hell wit' it all, me boy. . . to hell wit' it all."

He filled his glass to the brim. The bartender asked, "Have you seen the new glasses Hughie—they got sideboards on 'em."

The old man frowned.

"Shut yere damn mouth and spake whin yere spoken to—the glasses are little enough as 'tis—" was the irate answer.

Then aside to me, "Niver let yere infariors give ye any sass, me boy. If he were any good he wouldn't be servin' poison to the likes o' me." He laid a worn dime on the bar.

Old Hughie Tully was short and wide, with the strength of a bull.

My grandmother married him after she had inherited twenty acres of Irish ground.

With no money to buy horse and plow, they

tilled the land with spades. For five years they bent their backs and starved.

The adjoining land was owned by an English lord. They watched sleek horses furrow his acres with shining plows.

They sold the land to their aristocratic neighbor and came to America during the middle of the last century.

My grandfather was a peddler of Irish linens and laces in the South for three years.

His wandering had given him knowledge and contempt for people. In the South he often sent another Irishman to visit the town ahead of him. It was that man's duty to select a beautiful girl, and dress her in excellent laces and linens. In all her glory the maiden would go to mass on Sunday. All the other women would be curious to know where she purchased such fine raiment. The girl would tell them that she had met a peddler in a town nearby. Hughie, the adroit, would make his entrance in a few days and do a thriving business. His confederate would be in a town beyond making further arrangements.

[119]

"Wimmin are not all vain, indade not," his voice would raise, "some are dumb too."

My childhood was unusual in that it contained no soldier heroes. My grandfather had two distinct prejudices—he liked neither the Irish nor the negroes. His dislike of the former was based on general principles—and of the latter, because he believed that they were the souls of Methodists come back to earth—singed by hell-fire.

Believing this, he had no desire to fight for the freedom of scorched souls. The Civil War was deprived of his services.

I asked him why he had not been a soldier.

A man of nearly eighty then, his body still powerful, his sharp steel-blue eyes looking out from beneath shaggy eyebrows that had faded from red to yellowish gray, he snapped:

"If ye are in a strange nayborhood ye don't take sides—Ireland is me country—an' by the help of God may I niver see it agin!"

There was an old Irish shrew who did not like grandfather because he drank overmuch at times. She was haggard and worn. Her tongue was sharper than her features.

"The old hag, she said to me yisterday, 'Indade and if ye were me husband I'd give ye poison.'

" 'Indade and if I were, I'd take it,' I said right back."

Grandmother Tully was said to have been of better blood than he. The daughter of a country squire, she wrote verses.

Grandfather, who was never without his bottle, would often take a swig and exclaim:

"Sich blarney—makin' words jingle—indade—ye'd better be washin' the daishes."

When I told him I wanted to be a writer, he threw up his hands.

"Oh—me God, me God—git yereself a shovel like yere father—let yere grandmither do sich things—it's not for the likes of a brawny boy like ye."

When the rheumatism had forced grandfather to retire from a laborer's life to live on the sparse bounty of his children, he evolved a method that would keep an active mind from getting into a rut.

He would leave the house each morning at seven o'clock.

It was the hour the saloons opened.

There were twenty-six of them in St. Marys. Grandfather was the most charming of the village drunkards. He knew all the saloon keepers and bartenders in the place.

Many of them were Germans. Auglaize County was settled by Irish and German peasants. They were always at war.

Grandfather was the ambassador of love. Not for such a man were the squabbles of peasants.

He would lean his two hundred pound five-foot four body on the bar and pour soothing oil on the troubled waters of Irish and German— for a glass of liquor.

He was never really a cadger. He traded wit for drink. If wit were not needed, he gave consolation and advice. He had worn out several peddler's packs and many shovels. Thus equipped, he knew how to run the country, a neighbor's farm, and all affairs with women.

He was really a social appendage.

Every week he trimmed his black and white beard and mustache within a half-inch of his face.

He had never been to a dentist—had never lost a tooth. They were large and even.

He had retired at seventy.

"Indade—if a man works till three score and tin—an' rheumatiz taps at his heart an' no one kapes him—he'd better starve till they do."

His nose was large, his jaws heavy. He bit his words—between smiles.

There was only one negro in the town of St. Marys. In spite of his avowed prejudice, my grandfather was his bosom friend. The negro spent his money freely at the bar, which grandfather appreciated.

"Indade an' indade," grandfather often said to him, "a colored gintleman is better than the Irish—I know—for I'm one o' thim."

Often on the negro's day off, the two could be seen walking arm in arm from one saloon to the other.

My grandfather had a song which would make the darky laugh. He would pound the bar and stamp his feet to keep time, so he thought, with his words. All would listen.

"The Lord made a nayger,
He made him in the night,
He made him in sich a hurry,
He forgot to make him white."

Grandfather was one of the first men in Ohio to allow his wife complete expression. He would not bother her for days at a time. Unless, of course, liquor had made him slightly ill. He would then sit in his large chair and hit the table with his bottle.

"Kath-u-rin—Kath-u-rin," he would shout.

Grandmother, aged, stooped and vital, with wrinkles in her face deep enough to bury matches, would draw near him holding a corn-cob pipe in her hand.

"Indade, Kath-u-rin—you know what it is —it's that damned licker Coffee sells—it'd eat a hole in a pipe."

"Well, it's good for ye—a man yere age—

a-lettin' the licker soak yere fine brains out—
what'll iver become o' ye?"

"Be still, woman, be still—be still! It's
more licker I want an' not advice—indade a
woman o' ould Ireland should be ashamed to
talk so to her lord an' master."

"Indade an' ye'll git no more licker this
day!" was the defiant rejoinder.

At this insult grandfather would hurry from
the house.

But grandfather was unlike most men. Once
in the saloon, no one ever heard of his troubles
at home. He was a born man about town.

The saloon was his refuge from the crassness
of a peasant world into which he had been acci-
dentally born.

*   *   *   *   *   *   *

Grandfather loved the machinations of
politics. As a peddler he had learned to be a
great teller of tales. He could adapt himself to
any company. He could be droll or sentimental
by turns, according to his audience. He seemed
to read on faces the kind of story wanted. To

[125]

everyone in the town he was "Old Hughie."
But he was more than that—a traveling racon-
teur on the muddy road of life. He drank vile
and good liquor, and tried every means possible
to keep still-born the hopes that lay close to his
heart and brain.

At times, when alone with him, I could see
a pained expression on his face. And once,
when his immense shoulders ached when he
lifted the glass, he rested his hand on the
bar. . .

"Niver work hard wit' hands me boy—look
at me—I'm bint like an ould tree in the wind—
and for what—a bed that's niver made up—an'
shotgun whisky for a nickel a glass—an' the
damned rheumatiz on cold nights that cuts at
me flesh like Dick Hurm's razors. The praest'll
tell ye that work is noble—it may be—for a
mule—for he does none of it himself—I mane
the praest—.

"Now whin I was a pidler—" he sighed
deeply, and into his faded eyes came the pain of
happy memory, "ah thim were the days—even

the waeds along the road had blooms to thim
thin—

"Well—whin I was a pidler in Asheville—
it was a pimple on the world's nose thin—but
oh how purty—there was the swaytest little
yellow girls—with forms—" he curved his big
hands inward— "Ah me God—they were
lovely as sin—me wife was in Ireland thin—
an' would to Almighty God she had stayed there
—I could sing an' drink all night for a trainket
outta me pack—I always carried a trainket wit'
me—" He winked at the bartender—He
rubbed a left thumb and forefinger down a
heavy well shaped nose. His voice crooned—
"There was a little girl there—her dad had been
Irish—and he missed mass one Sunday an'
sinned wit' her mother—an' later on—he left
the holy church—her eyes were as a flower on
a plate—an' her skin was brown an' soft like a
berry in the sun—I've niver known anything
like her—I give her four pieces of lace one
time—her father was an old pidler who lived
in mortal sin—he opened a store in Nashville—
and I says to him I says—'Ah the purty little

[127]

maid in Ashville—and ye know she's yours'—
and he says—'Which one, Hughie—I'm an old
man—'tis hard to remimber—'

"I'd attinded his dear wife's funeral that day
—he rode so sad to the graveyard—it was all
I could do to take the bottle out of his hands—
there was little left for me to drown of the
agony of death—an' on the way home from the
dear woman's grave he stopped an' picked up
the purtiest woman ye iver see—an' he married
her right off an' took her to his house—an' he
met Moses the Jew who ran a store in the nixt
block nixt to him. . .

"An' Moses said, 'Who is she?'

" 'An' who would she be'—says he—'I'm an
honorable man an' I obey the laws of me
country an' me God—she's me wife ye fool—
I'm a better trader than ye—I've traded a dead
one for a live one. . .'

"But his daughter—how be-utiful—she
didn't have a brain in her head—as no woman
should—but she could make a poor sad pidler
forgit Holy Communion at the hour of his
death—ah—a man of miny loves is always a

[128]

sad man—that's the pain of it—but it's all ye have lift in the ind—an' niver kape thim too long—they git old an' faded—the stalk when the rose is gone—oh well—I thought I'd niver get out of Asheville—I had to walk two nights to make up on me route—but I wint back agin —an' agin—that's long ago now—fifty years maybe—"

He looked down at his right foot which rested on the brass railing. . . "Yis—yis— that's long iver ago now—she died of the consoomption."

The bartender laughed. The old man looked sternly at him.

"The likes o' ye would laugh at the spaych of your bitters," he said quickly. "I'll spind me other four nickels ilsewhere."

We left the saloon.

Owing, no doubt to his three wandering years as a peddler, my grandfather knew the locations of towns and villages everywhere in America. He also knew which mercantile commodities were most in use in that section.

He was at heart a politician. He had been an election tout in the South. For a fee, he adroitly told of a candidate's many good qualities across a state.

His memory was tenacious. It retained, as if in a vise, the tiniest incident.

He could play a fiddle and sing a ballad.

Walking vagabonds with fiddles would often play in Ohio saloons. Old Hughie would take the fiddle and help entertain until, and often long after, the saloon closed. He had picked up stray negro tunes in the south. I can still hear the magnificent old lover of life chanting with terrific gusto—

"I wish I waaz an apple—
An' my yaller gal waaz anither
An' O—how happee we would be—
On the tree together—

"Oh how jealous the niggahs would be—
When by my side they spied her—
An' oh how happee we would be—
All smashed up into cider—

[130]

"*One day we lubbed along the ribber—*
An' de win' blew kinda hard—
Till it made my little Dinah shibber—
Just like some new made lard—

"*An' wit' her little hips a-quibber —*
Into my arms I caught her—
An' when the win' blew up again—
It blew us in the water—

"*An' she stayed right on close to me—*
Her little hips a-quibber—
Dat I forgot mos' happily—
Dat I was in de ribber—

"*An' dey took my Dinah on de shore—*
An' sabed her from de drowned—
An' I had to swim around' some moah—
Foh me dey nebber found—"

The happy crowd would buy him many
drinks. It was a tacit understanding between
bartenders and old Hughie that when other
people treated him that the liquor was to be of

the best. Whether he drank five hours or ten, Hughie Tully never lost control of his senses. Liquor merely made him more alive and charming. It made him forget the shovel and the ditch and the wretched cottage in which he passed as few hours as possible.

A keen old actor; he knew how to play upon the moods of people.

The little yellow fiddle seemed a toy with the immense arms about it. The red flannel undershirt was rolled to the elbows. The great muscles of his forearms bulged like pieces of broken whipcord. Now the old man was really in his element. His hair, like withered gray wild grass, was in a heap of tangles on his head. The vagabond fiddlers, glad of a recess, entered into the spirit of each song. Old Hughie took all the drinks offered. But when the hat was passed, all the money went to the strolling players.

There was a path reserved at the end of the bar where Hughie's glass and bottle stood. The entertainer had need of drink after each song. No man ever stood in that path.

The bartender would raise his hand. Many hands would be raised. Old Hughie was to sing again. His manner was that of a man whom no one dared to disturb. With squat heavy body tense, his head hung low, his lips held tight and firm, he would move toward the bar and pour himself a glass brimful of Three Star Hennessy while the crowd watched expectant.

Then with heavy resonant voice he would begin. . .

"Look down, look down—dat lonesome road—
  Hang—you head—an' cri—ee—
  De best ob friends—must hab to pa—ht—
  So why not—you an' I—ee—"

The voice clutched everything hard from every face. They went soft like children's.

The fiddle crooned low. Men entering the saloon were swept into the mood at once. They walked softly.

"True love—true love—what have I done—
  That you should treat me—so—?

[133]

You caused me joy I had wit' you—
Like I nevah had befoah—

"Look down—look down—at lonesome
road—
Hang youah head—an' cri—ee—
De best ob friends must hab to pa—ht—
So why not you—an' I—ee—."

Applause and drinking followed.

Old Hughie suddenly shifted the mood. He handed the fiddle to the strolling vagabond. Clapping his hands on his knees, feet keeping time on the floor, he chanted. . .

"Moses an' Noah went to jail—
But de ark kep' floatin' on—
De Lawd came down and went dere bail—
An' de ark kep' floatin' on—

" 'Whaddye mean,' said de Lawd mos' high—
While de ark kep' rollin' on—
'If you don't behave I'll bust you in de eye—
While de ark kep' rollin' on—

[134]

" 'For I've got a whole lot moah to do—
Dan keep dis ark a floatin'—
I gotta keep track ob de Wanderin' Jew
An' kep dis ark afloatin'—' "

No one ever knew where he learned the many stories he told. But he always had a new tale to tell.

"Did ye iver hear of the man who drank too much? Well, he worried his wife till she went to the praist wit' her troubles. 'Father,' she says—'he drinks like a well—an' no prayers of me own can stop him.'

"The praist heard her wit' a button off his cassock.

" 'Wait'—says the holy man—' 'tis I that will stop him an' put the fear of Almighty God in his heart.'

"So that night he wint to Michael who was so dhrunk he thought he was the Black Pope.

" 'Michael'—says the holy father—'if the good Lord answers yere prayers will ye quit dhrinkin!'

[135]

" 'Yis'—says Michael—'I'll be quittin' even if his mother answers thim.'

" 'All right,' says the praist—'we'll pray to the Blissed Virgin.'

" 'An' what will ye ask her'—asks the praist.

" 'I'll ask her'—says the dhrunken scoundrel —'For the loan of tin dollars.'

" 'All right'—says the holy father—'go ahead and ask the Holy Mother for tin dollars.'

"Michael knilt on the hard road with the praist at his side.

" 'Swate Virgin, Mither of a man without min—' he said— 'may the prayer of a poor bedraggled soul wantin' the loan of tin dollars float up to ye and into the corridors of heaven —it is only tin dollars I would be havin' an' it's me first chance to iver git so much money out of a virgin woman—'

"The praist felt in his coat pocket. There was only four dollars. The praist forgot for a minute. Then he put the four dollars in Michael's coat pocket.

" 'Feel in yere pocket, Michael,' says the

praist—'An' see if yere prayers be not answered.'

"Michael felt in his pocket and drew out four dollars.

"He looked at the money dolefully.

" 'Did she give ye the tin?' asked the praist.

" 'No, begorra—' says Michael—'she owes me six dollars yit.'

" 'Well, she'll pay that aisy'—says the holy father— 'just remember it an' lo an' behold— some day the Blessed Mither will remimber it too—an' pay you in the gold she scrapes off the stars on Aister Sunday.' "

The old man chuckled.

"Michael got dhrunk on the four dollars.

"The woman hurried to the praist agin.

"The good man waited for Michael to come home late at night. A white sheet was about the Holy Father's head as he stood behind a tree in the road. As Michael came along singin',

" 'It's the purtiest God damn country that iver yit was seen—

[137]

*Where they're hangin' min an' wimen for the
wearin' o' the green!'* "

"An' who should step right out but a ghost
from behind the trae.

"Michael shivered at first an' was afraid to
run so he became brave.

" 'An' who may ye be?' he asked, his taith
rattlin' like stones in his mouth.

"The ghost answered in a voice dayper than
thunder in London.

" *'I'm Jasus Christ.'*

"Michael was relieved right away, away.

"He held the ghost in his arms. . .

" 'Oh, I'm so glad to see you', he said—an'
he held him close—

" 'Yere mither owes me six dollars—' "

CHAPTER XII

THE WAKE

LITERALLY a swamp was that section of Ohio in which my relatives settled. It was an abiding place for mosquitoes and ditch diggers.

Men became proficient with the pick and shovel more than eighty years ago. At that time the St. Marys reservoir was completed. It is perhaps the most dismal sheet of water that ever stretched muddy malarial waves under the sun. About ten miles long and from four to eight miles wide, it remains ever the same.

The moon throws a sad light of beauty over the still water. And that is all. It is turned then, by a glorious transformation into a floor of gold.

Clouds hang above it during the hot months as if too listless to move. But in my bedraggled boyhood they were many colored castles of the sky. Hot winds would tear them apart and send

[139]

them slowly over the sky. They would soon reunite.

The reservoir, in its natural state, was a prairie and a forest. It was formed by the raising of two walls to the east and west. They were several miles in length. The natural elevation to the north and south then formed a basin which retained the water.

It is used as a feeder for sixty miles of the Miami Canal. It rolls in muddy waves into the Maumee River at Defiance.

Wild fowl often gathered in the spring and summer of the year. They brought a touch of beauty to the dismal lake. Most of them were shot by the citizens of Ohio. The rest flew away to wilder and grander scenes. They never returned.

The sun has burned the bark from drowned trees, which project, smooth as boards, from the stagnant water. Those scavengers of still water, the carp, thrive on decayed vegetable matter. In earlier summers the odor from the dreary lake was enough to drive even the Irish away.

The Legislature passed a law which made it compulsory to remove all timber from the site of the proposed reservoir. It appropriated many thousands of dollars for the purpose. The law was not heeded. The water was turned in on a forest of trees. The money was squandered elsewhere.

Scores of farms had not been paid for by the state when the reservoir was completed. The water rolled over growing crops of wheat and corn.

A public meeting was held.

State officials were warned that the bank would be cut through. The reply came back. . . . "The guards will rout you."

Then several hundred citizens, armed with picks and shovels, in two days tore a vast hole through the embankment. Men quarreled for the chance to be the first to turn the water loose. It soon hurled fifty yards below.

Six weeks passed before the water subsided.

Warrants were issued for judges, county officials and leading citizens engaged in the work. No grand jury could be found that would return an indictment against them.

Farms and roadways needed ditches which drained toward the reservoir. Often large creeks, many miles long, were dug with horses and scrapers through woods and fields. Tile ditches were laid across farms. Open ditches were dug along the roads. At this hard labor, my grandfather early trained on the bogs of Ireland, became expert. He early taught my father who was rated as the best "open ditch man" in Auglaize, Van Wert, Paulding and Mercer counties. Not a week passed in fifty years that my father had not a shovel in his hands. He lived at lonely farm houses in the four counties named, contracting the digging of ditches at so much a yard. Saturday afternoon and Sunday he would spend at a saloon in a nearby town.

If the town were fifteen miles away and the mud ankle deep, he would walk. He never asked any man for a ride. Like a gorilla he would swing his mightily-muscled body over the mud.

My grandfather was a better "tile ditch

man" than my father. This required more painstaking labor. The ditch, from three to five feet deep, slanted downward slightly, according to the length of land which needed draining. The tile, which measured from six to twelve inches across, would be laid carefully, like a red stove pipe under the ground.

The work would be done in rain and wind. Old Hughie, mud bespattered, a stub pipe in his mouth, which in working hours was never lit, could dig a tile ditch straight across a meadow without the slightest deviation.

He would eat his dinner from a tin bucket in the open field. A compartment for liquid into which a cup was fitted, was at the top of the bucket. Black coffee was not alone used in the tin compartment. An equal portion of whisky was mixed with it.

Garrulous often, the old man was strangely silent at work. In summer or winter his sleeves were always rolled up.

A light eater at midday, he would throw most of his lunch to the birds. He always rested a half hour. During this time he would slowly

drink his whisky-flavored coffee; as though it
were something to be enjoyed.

Like my father, there was in him no sentimentality. In spite of the long streams of
ignorance and superstition which ran in their
blood, each man had a faculty of seeing beyond
the surface of life. That is perhaps why they
drank so much.

With limitations over which they had no
control, they were callous-handed but tactful
connoisseurs of life.

No man could insult either of them in a
public gathering.

Once my grandfather was called a son of
a bitch. The epithet has caused murder to be
committed. Men waited. The old man
shrugged his shoulders—"Well—well," he
smiled, "a bitch or a woman—what matter?"

The man who had offered the supposed insult
bought plenty of liquor for the old diplomat
that day.

Breweries and distilleries were plentiful in
Ohio. Saloon keepers paid their bills every
two weeks. Collectors for Cincinnati breweries,

generally large good natured German men, visited St. Marys regularly.

My grandfather knew just when each man would arrive. They all knew him by name.

Each saloon keeper was glad to have plenty of customers in the place when the collector called. When the bill was paid, the collector always treated the house several times. If no one were in the place the saloon keeper lost money.

Old Hughie Tully, always glad to help his friends and himself, would make the rounds of the saloons with the collectors.

It was an unwritten law never to drink whisky when a collector for a brewery treated.

But the old man made his own laws.

"Indade," he used to say to them, "it's a man I am, an' not a barrel—let the Germans dhrink the sthuff—it's nothin' but yellow water anyhow."

With this pronouncement he would drink the best grade of whisky all day long.

Other men would fall by the wayside before the collector had received half the money due

[145]

him. Old Hughie, faithful to the last, would never miss a drink.

Often the collector would visit for an hour or more in an important saloon. If my grandfather were engaged in conversation when the collector was ready to leave, he would always call:

"Come on Hughie,"

Together they would walk to the next saloon.

Every now and then as a compliment to the beer collector, the old man would expostulate on the merits of beer. Pointing a shovel twisted fore-finger he would say loudly: "Sh—ure—an' beer is good for the health. There was a man over in Lima who had tumors bigger than balloons. He started to dhrinkin' beer an' they all wint away."

"Why don't you drink it then—" the collector would ask.

"Indade an' I have no tumors, glory be to God—I dhrank it whin I was a young man in Dooblin—but whin the famine came I told Almighty God if he'd be so thoughtful as to save me I'd niver dhrink another dhrop—unless I had tumors. I kept my word—but I'm damned glad I didn't make it whisky. Indade I'd sooner of died in the famine . . ."

Hughie was always accompanied by William Webb. I have changed his name for fear that his family might remember him. His face was heavy and red with laughter. His paunch shook far in front of him as he walked. A bachelor, he was an habitué of St. Marys saloons for thirty years.

He died at last of delirium tremens. Old Hughie walked across the town on a blizzardy night in December. His heavy feet crunched the snow. The intense cold drove the rheumatism deeper into his bones. But a drinking comrade was reported dying of the D.T.'s. He had yelled in his delirium for my grandfather.

Old Hughie often told of the time when Webb had wounded a burglar.

"Did ye shoot him in self defense?" asked the sheriff.

"Indade and I didn't," answered Webb. "I shot him in the rump jist as he was gittin' over the fence."

[147]

Webb was tearing at the bed clothing and throwing snakes out of the window, when Hughie entered his little cottage.

"God, Hughie—they're after me—chase 'em off, chase 'em off—they're bigger than whales—ah—ah!—ah!! There's one on the bed."

My grandfather sat near the bed as a doctor gave the snake-demented bachelor a hypodermic. Then William Webb shut his eyes, opened his mouth, stretched his three hundred pounds across the bed and lay forever still.

"It's jist as well," commented old Hughie— "Whin a man can't carry his dhrink like a gintleman it's time to go to the arms of Jaysus who dhrank only wine."

Money was scarce that winter in St. Marys. Funerals were many. A saloon-keeper advanced enough to bury Webb.

Old Hughie had said to Webb's friends: "It's bist we have a wake for the dare old frind— we that were his frinds should niver disert him in the hour of his death."

Crasby, Hughie and others of the pious, laid

Webb on a table after the body had been washed.

"Handle him keerful," said Hughie—"for he'll soon be dirthy enough in the ground."

They laid him out with black ribbons tied about him.

"Oh God," said Crasby, "he wasn't married —and it's white ribbons for them that are not."

"Be sthill," flared old Hughie—"He's married to the Blissed Virgin forever—and worry he'll not about the color of a ribbon."

Whisky and food in abundance for the occasion was furnished by several saloon keepers.

Lighted candles were placed on the table about Webb, who lay, a mountain of flesh towering in the middle. His hands seemed to fold with an effort across his breast, so short were his heavy arms.

Three old women soon entered. They were the keeners, or professional mourners for the dead—for a fee.

They looked at the body now with eyes full of tears.

"Oh—why did he die?" they asked in unison. "Oh—why did he die?"

"It's too early to ask that!" retorted old Hughie—"there's some more people comin'."

For Hughie and the German saloon keepers had allowed the news to be spread about that Webb was to have a wake.

Many men left the saloons early. Others came later.

The rooms of death were crowded.

It was thought best not to ask the priest to attend with prayers for the dead.

Old Hughie retired to another room with some bosom friends and the whisky.

Crasby received the guests.

"There's no wakes in Ameriky like them we had in Ireland," began Old Hughie, when the bottles were opened.

"They used to gather in Ireland before the man died like a lot o' happy buzzards—Glory be to God."

He chuckled.

"It was like a show—an' the payple would come from far off to see it. An' they'd always buy the licker an' the grub for what with so many wakes an' one thing an' another, the payple in Ireland were poor—

"An' one time two Englishers wanted a wake —as though they hadn't seen enough o' the Irish dead—an' Paddy Fitzpatrick was sick an' he wasn't dyin'. So we got Paddy to play dead for the dear English who bought the whisky.

"An' they all come—an' the keeners cried— an' he lay there like the good actor he was— until one o' the Englishers put the hot ind of a cigar on the cold ind of Paddy's nose—"

Old Hughie drank and chuckled.

"An' Paddy rose from the dead quicker thin Lazrus—an' he wint bounden outta the room as though a lump o' hell fire had fell on him.

"He took the shroud wit' him—an' away he flew over the hills an' the bogs.

"Thin the Irish got mad because the English had sacrileged the dead—an' they run thim over the hills an' the bogs too—the poor shports."

Soon the cottage was full. The Irish dread the thought of death perhaps more than any other race. This may explain their seeming contempt of the dismal collector.

Laughter and jokes were everywhere about the big shell that had once been Webb.

Jack Raley was there. He had been working as a printer on a newspaper in Lima. He had come, not to bury Webb, but to drink liquor at his wake.

It was the duty of the keeners to learn the biography of the man who was dead.

This learned, they would chant his good deeds through the house.

Always would they end with the question— "Oh—why did he die?"

A group of Germans were gathered about a barrel of beer which had been tapped under an apple tree. Two lanterns hung above it.

They were the friends of the leading German contributor of liquor.

Soon the voices of the keeners were heard. At first they were faint—quavering old women in tears. Then they rose in a witches' unison.

Tight black gowns over bony wrinkled bodies, they clenched their hands on their breasts.

One stood at Webb's head, one on each side.

The candles spurted about the dead drunkard who died of exhaustion while running away from snakes.

Old Hughie, John Crasby, Jack Raley, and their friends crowded into the room.

As if tired of the pose, the hands of William Webb had come slightly apart.

Jack Raley folded them again.

"He was niver one to pray for long," grinned my grandfather.

"Not if there wasn't a dhrink comin'," smiled Jack Raley.

"May his soul rist in peace," put in John Crasby.

"Why wish him thet?" asked Hughie. "There's no dhrinks where there's peace."

The voices of the keeners rose in a terrifying wail.

Tears for one for whom they cared not rolled down their old cheeks.

Their gray sparse hair became disheveled with the weeping.

"Oh—why—did—he—die?"

"Oh—why—did—he—die?"

[153]

"He was good to the poor—he prayed for the souls in purgatory—he helped the fallen women—

"Oh why did he die?"

"Oh why did he die?"

They walked in a circle about the body of the drunkard.

"He gave alms to the church—"

They hesitated, in trying to remember the good qualities of Webb. They repeated—

"He gave alms to the church."

A voice yelled in imitation of the keeners—

"He had a big belly—"

"Oh why did he die?

"Oh why did he die?"

The keeners stopped for a moment.

"Go on—don't let no irrireverence like that interfere," advised Old Hughie. "It's the business of nobody's because he had a big belly—"

"He should o' used it for beer an' the snakes wouldn't o' got after him," muttered Jack Raley to my grandfather.

The keeners cried:

"He wint to confession—

[154]

"He ate no mate on Friday—
"Oh why did he die?
"Oh why did he die?"
A man under the apple tree yelled—
"He never missed a drink!"
My grandfather grinned.
"It's thim Germans—they have no respect for the dead."
"Oh why did he die?
"Oh why did he die?"
The body of William Webb slowly began to rise. His hands fell apart. His arms remained still and bent like a mummy's.
At first no one noticed.
His face had risen at least a foot before a keener shrieked and ran from the room. William Webb continued rising.
At last he sat erect in his shroud—glassy eyes staring. People ran screaming in all directions. Some jumped out of the windows.
A German saloon-keeper ran directly into the barrel which he had contributed.
"He's come to life," he shouted, "he's gittin' up!"

[155]

Never did Germans and Irish run so swiftly.

They struck the middle of a deserted street, their heavy feet pounding.

The contributor of beer, with a belly larger than the late Webb's, led the retreating revellers.

Suddenly there swished by them three black forms.

The three old keeners were on their way home.

A half hour later Old Hughie, Jack Raley and John Crasby walked slowly homeward. They carried two quarts of whisky each.

"Well, well, well," commented old Hughie, "Webb would laugh at that one. I thought the whisky would be gone before it happened."

"Yis—and so did I," returned Raley, "I niver had sich a job—the cellar was dark an' we pushed and pushed—it was like raisin' a horse."

"Will ye be up in time for the funeral, Hughie?" John Crasby asked.

"Oh yis—the bist we can do for him that's gone is to show respect an' go early."

A flat board had been placed under Webb's back. A long thin pole was attached to the board. A hole was drilled through the floor. It was raised from the cellar.

* * * * * * *

Funeral corteges often stopped at an outlying saloon on the way to the cemetery. No flowers had been purchased for Webb. Too late the sad oversight had been discovered.

"An' why do ye want flowers?" asked Old Hughie. "He didn't know one from a waid— an' he niver kin see thim now."

"But it's respectful—don't you see—you wouldn't want to be tumbled in the ground without nobody thinkin' of you would you?" Jack Raley asked Old Hughie.

"Shure—I wouldn't give niver a damn— they don't aven nade to bury me if they don't wanta."

Just then a group from another funeral cortege stopped at the saloon.

"The Lord be praised—business is good," said my grandfather.

The new arrivals lined up at the bar and ordered whisky.

Old Hughie looked out of the saloon door at the other hearse. Inside was a coffin covered with wreaths of flowers. He opened the hearse door and took two wreaths and laid them on Webb's coffin.

"If it's flowers the poor divil nades—it's flowers he shall have," he said.

He returned to the saloon.

Soon the different corteges went their way.

Old Hughie breathed hard against the frosted window of the carriage. . . . Inside were seated the four leading topers of the town.

"I wonder if William went to heaven," said John Crasby, rubbing the red bulb on the end of his nose.

"Shure," returned my grandfather—"where in the divil else would he go. For if iver they put 'im in hell the alkihol in him would make the fire too hot for Old Nick himself."

"So you believe in hell?" asked Crasby.

"I do for a man who can't hold his licker.

I'd sind me own son there if he failed me in that."

"Well he won't fail you," put in Crasby.

"No—he's been brung up like a man," said my grandfather.

The hearse stopped. The pall bearers carried all but the memory of Webb to the grave.

Old Hughie carried the two wreaths of flowers.

The undertaker rubbed his hands reverently. It was very cold. He scanned the inscriptions on the cards attached to the flowers. One read:

"To my darling mother asleep in Jesus."

Upon the other card were the words:

"To my devoted wife these forty-two years."

"R.I.P."

Old Hughie looked at the letters and frowned.

"He called her a rip," he said.

CHAPTER XIII

A STRANGER HOME FROM THE WARS

SAVE that he had a greater sense of drama, Old Hughie Tully was like a popular novelist. He gave his audience what it wanted.

He often began a story with "whin I was a pidler in the South——" After these words he would look about in the manner of a man who expected silence. It generally followed. He would then look from his empty glass to the bartender. More liquor was poured.

"You know gintlemen—when I was a pidler in the South——"

All were ready for the story. A drunken man entered, with a wooden leg.

"Please gentlemen," he pleaded, "be so kind as to contribute money toward the expense of another wooden leg. I lost my leg at the battle of Bull Run aholdin' back the rebel hordes from the fair valleys of the North."

Old Hughie looked sternly at the newcomer.

[160]

The intrusion was unwarranted. "Who is the gintleman?" he asked.

"Oh—some one-legged hobo—they're always drunk," returned John Crasby.

Old Hughie began again. "When I was a pidler in the South." The voice rose higher —"Gentlemen—will you help an old man who lost a leg in humblin' his country's pride. I was the fastest runner at the battle of Bull Run, gentlemen. It was me that got General Jackson the name of Stonewall, gentlemen. He was gallopin' like hell on his horse with General Lee's daughter holdin' to him and I came dashin' by. General Lee yells out—'That Yank's goin' so fast he makes Jackson look like a stone wall.' "

Grandfather Tully looked at him, with grim wrinkles of laughter about his eyes.

The man's leg was off above the knee. A piece of wood was fastened to it. It was like no other wooden leg ever made. Worn wood curved around an iron band at the bottom. His upper lip was shaved clean. His jaws were covered with bright red whiskers that hung at

least a dozen inches and spread across his breast.
His eyes were full of laughter. One forgot his
thin upper lip in looking at them. He wore a
heavy blue army coat which had brass buttons.
Several brass medals half hidden by the whiskers, hung from the left side of his breast. They
shone bright from the constant rubbing of hair
upon them. His hair, perhaps once red, was of
an indescribable color.

An old army hat was crumpled on his head.
Several holes were torn through the crown.

He was very tall and very drunk. Whenever
he took a step, the wooden leg crashed upon the
floor with a resounding thud.

Old Hughie Tully looked away from him.

He began once again: "Now whin I was a
pidler in the South—" The one-legged man
faced my grandfather.

"Do you live in this town?" he asked.

Old Hughie rubbed his stubby whiskers.
He looked slightly perturbed. "Indade—if it
plazes yure insolence to know—I do." The
man with the wooden leg gazed with unconcern
at a picture of Falstaff drinking beer.

Old Hughie, still nettled, snapped the words at his questioner. "And why did ye ask?"

"Oh—for no reason at all," returned the man, throwing his left hand upward, "You just looked like a man who *would* live here."

"I look like a bright man—I'd be for sayin'!" flared Old Hughie.

"Well maybe you do—but you deceive your looks," came back the man with one leg.

"Say—who the livin' hell are you?"

"I'm a soldier, sir—home from the wars. The hero of battles never forgot—the inventor of unshed tears." He pulled his whiskers aside.

"See these medals. I won them all. I am he that runs. It was my old friend Napoleon who said, 'Give the fools medals'—but strange to say though, I'm a Union soldier, I won mine by getting Jackson a new name. Jefferson Davis said to George Washington that a man who can run like that deserves to be treated well. . ."

He laid a nickel on the bar. "Give me a mug of beer, bartender please." The foaming liquid was placed before him.

[163]

"But gentlemen guzzlers, I digress—I would feign recite ere I inhale the amber fluid—

"Be so kind each and all to give me your attention—it will repay you well and give you a view of whisky drinkers on their way to the torment they have so richly earned—"

Striking the attitude of Bryan at a rustic gathering he began—

"An Irish mick on a barroom floor,
Drunk so much he could hold no more;
He fell asleep with a troubled brain,
To dream that he rode on the hell-bound train.

"The engine with human blood was damp,
The head light was a brimstone lamp,
An imp for fuel was shoveling bones,
And the furnace roared with a thousand groans.

"The tank was filled with lager beer,
The devil himself was engineer,
The passengers were a mixed-up crew—
Churchman, atheists, Baptist, Jew.

[164]

"*The rich in broadcloth, poor in rags,*
  Handsome girls and wrinkled hags;
  Black men, yellow, red and white,
  Chained together—fearful sight.

"*The train rushed on at awful pace,*
  And sulphur fumes burned hands and face;
  Wilder and wilder the country grew,
  Fast and faster the engine flew.

"*Loud and terrible thunder crashed,*
  White, brighter lightning flashed;
  Hotter still the air became,
  Till clothes were burned from each shrinking
        frame.

"*Then came a fearful ear-splitting yell,*
  Yelled Satan, "Gents, the next stop's Hell!"
  'Twas then the passengers shrieked with pain,
  And begged the devil to stop the train."

The gathering pressed closer to the man who begged for a leg.

The veteran grabbed at the glass from which the foam had gone.

"Bartender—put a head on it."

The bartender poured more beer into the mug. The stranger blew the foam on the bar.

"Precious fluid—Balm in Gilead for us whose hearts are heavy from lost loves and present hates." He slammed the empty mug on the bar.

"Now gentlemen—listen closely—I'll show you the devil himself and let you pinch his tail. He began again with terrifying gusto—

"He shrieked and roared and grinned with glee,
And mocked and laughed at their misery,
'My friends, you've bought your seats on this
road,
I've got to go through with the awful load.'"

He turned to my grandfather.

" 'You've bullied the weak, you've cheated the
poor,
The starving tramp you've turned from the
door,
You've laid up gold till your purses bust,
You've given play to your beastly lust.

[166]

" 'You've mocked at God in your hell-born
     pride,
  You've killed and you've cheated; you've
     plundered and lied,
  You've double-crossed men and you've sworn
     and you've stole,
  Not one but has perjured his body and soul.' "

"Turn yere head away from me," shouted
Old Hughie, as the stranger continued.

" 'So you've paid full fare and I'll carry you
     through,
  If there's one don't belong, I'd like to know
     who.
  And here's the time when I ain't no liar,
  I'll land you safe in the land of fire.

" 'There your flesh will scorch in the flames
     that roar,
  You'll sizzle and scorch from rind to core.'
  Then the mick he woke with a thrilling cry,
  His clothes were wet and his hair stood high.

"And he prayed as he never until that hour,
  To be saved from hell and the devil's power.
  His prayers and his vows were not in vain
  And he paid no fare on the hell-bound train."

The audience gasped when the speaker finished. They looked at one another as though a preacher were among them.

"He's crazier'n a whole asylum," Old Hughie volunteered to John Crasby.

"He'll land in the calaboose if he keeps that up," was Crasby's comment.

"Bartender, won't you wet the speaker's whistle, please?" The bartender filled the mug.

The stranger drank it quickly, and rubbed his lower lip slightly.

"See that upper lip," he said to the bartender, "I was years in learning to get rid of my mustache. It hindered my beer drinking. At last, came wisdom and I had it shaved off. So long does it take us to learn the simple things." He sighed. "Men grow old and die before they learn how to drink a glass of beer."

[168]

Hearing the man talk to the bartender, Old Hughie began once more, "Whin I was a pidler in the South . . ."

The one-legged man waved his arms.

"But, gentlemen—I would speak to you one and all. I am a wounded veteran long run home from the wars. May I ask a small collection from this august assembly. I am endeavoring as becomes the pride of a soldier—to get a new leg. So long as the great heroes of the Civil War lived, I was well supplied with the money for new legs. But now they are all gone—one by one they have joined, unwilling as they may have been, the bivouac of the dead."

He thumped his leg on the floor.

Skeletons of valor under dead roses—fools dying for fools. Oh I am sad for dead heroes—

"For ah—

"*By the flow of the inland river,*
Whence the fleets of iron have fled,
Where the blades of grave-grass quiver,
Asleep are the ranks of the dead:—

[169]

"Under the sod and the dew,
Waiting the Judgment Day:—
Under the one, the Blue;
Under the other, the Gray.

"These in the robings of glory,
These in the gloom of defeat,
All with battle-blood gory,
In the dusk of eternity meet:—

"Under the sod and the dew,
Waiting the Judgment Day:—
Under the laurel, the Blue:
Under the willow, the Gray."

"Lord, what a lot of mush," Old Hughie said to John Crasby.

"Maybe he'll be still now. Surely he can't talk after sich folly-de-rol."

The stranger remained pensive, as if living over again the days when he vanished from glory. He suddenly drained his mug of beer.

"Whin I was a pidler in the South," Old Hughie looked at his audience. They moved closer. "As I wuz sayin'—Whin I was a pid—"

The veteran shouted:

"Gentlemen who wave flags on the Fourth of July—I—a one-legged soldier—who retreated from Moscow with Napoleon—who has ever been far in the forefront in the wars of humanity—even though in that cause I have become legless—I ask the boon of a new leg."

The swinging doors of the saloon opened and shut.

A group of well-dressed men entered. They were lead by Barney Russell, collector for a Kentucky distillery.

"Bellies to the bar, men," he called, "bellies to the bar."

Soon all in the place were lined up at the bar for a drink. All took whisky but the one-legged man. He asked for a large glass of beer. "The nerve of a man like that," said John Crasby.

"Yis—" said Old Hughie, "only a hobo would act so ungrateful."

Exasperated, Hughie said to the stranger,

[171]

"What do you mane—dhrinkin' beer on a man who sills whisky?"

The one-legged man rubbed his upper lip and looked at my grandfather a moment.

"Do you know how Rockyfeller got rich?" he asked quietly.

"No—I do not," replied old Hughie, nonplused.

"It was very simple," replied the man, "he merely tended to his own business."

Old Hughie swallowed twice.

"You are not a man I should pay attintion to —I don't aven know you."

The stranger returned: "Neither does any man—I turn on daylight each morning—I clip the wings of angels if they fly too high—I started the myth that peace could be had in the world—" His eyes looked narrow at old Hughie. "If you knew me, my friend—you would not numb the shriveled worms in your skull with whisky—it is a drink for savages and saints."

The bartender filled the glasses a second time.

Russell was busy counting the bills which the

saloon keeper handed him. Satisfied with the amount he called, "Fill 'em up again." The glasses were filled the third time.

The one-legged soldier swallowed his beer before Old Hughie and John Crasby raised their glasses. He wiped his shaven upper lip again and turned to my grandfather, saying:

"This is what you ought to have—a lip like this—no beer lost. I figured it all out. Eighty-eight barrels of beer stuck to my mustache before I had brains enough to shave it off. It's the little things that count in beer drinking. My father was a brew-master in Poland. I worked in a brewery there until I was forty years old. I learned the beer business from the suds down."

"Was that before you wint to the war," asked Old Hughie.

"It was all during the wars," the reply came quickly.

Old Hughie shook his head. The soldier looked at him.

"You know, stranger," explained the one-legged man, "the drinking of beer is a lost art

[173]

in this country or rather it is an art which barbaric whisky guzzlers have not learned." He looked hard at my grandfather. "Now my father, after he returned from Siberia as brewmaster to the Czar of Tasmania, explained to me that beer should never be tasted with the tongue—it should be swallowed—"

"Like castor oil," put in Old Hughie.

"Or whisky—or any other medicine for children," returned the soldier from Bull Run.

"Men should never drink beer out of glasses. Heavy mugs should be used to hold the tongue out of the beer. There's a great art in drinking beer." He felt his chest proudly.

"How about whisky," asked my grandfather.

"You pour it on the kindling and strike a match to it."

"Gwan—" Hughie's words were stopped in his throat.

"I've never been able to understand," said the stranger, looking straight at my grandfather, "how men drink whisky. One may as well eat matches for breakfast and drink nitroglycerine."

The crowd laughed.

"Do ye know how Rockyfeller got rich?" my grandfather asked.

"Su-re—in the oil business," the stranger replied.

My grandfather looked crestfallen.

"He had his mind on bigger things than beer drinkin' anyhow."

The wooden-legged man drained his mug. With one eye closed he remarked:

"I just heard a good one."

"What is it?" asked my grandfather.

"It's a riddle."

"Well go ahead," said Old Hughie, anxiously.

"What is it that stands on one leg and barks like a dog?"

Old Hughie thought long and earnestly.

"Give up?" asked the stranger.

"Yis—"

"It's a stork."

"But a stork don't bark like a dog," returned old Hughie peevishly.

"Oh well—that's just to make it harder."

[175]

"Well, I'll be sint to purgatory for mortal sin!" snapped Old Hughie.

The stranger chased a fly from his upper lip and roared in a voice of thunder:

"As I turned down the new cut road—
I met old Nick with a devil of a load.
And I said, 'Satan—please do tell—
They're a lot o' whisky topers on their way to
  hell.'"

A roar of laughter went through the saloon. When it had subsided, the collector said:

"Give that fellow a lot of beer on me."

The bartender placed three mugs before the wandering soldier.

While the stranger regaled himself, Old Hughie looked at the smiling faces—

"When I was a pidler in the South—"

The stranger looked up from three empty mugs.

His voice drowned Old Hughie's like turbulent water.

"I'll never forget the time I was coming

[176]

from Ethiopa with my father. He'd con-
structed a brewery over there for Booker T.
Washington and he took me with him. On the
way back we boarded a frozen ship. You never
saw another one like it. Its sails were always on
fire. Big splashes of flame kept dropping into
the ocean and sizzling the water. The ship was
burning up and melting at the same time. The
sailors skated around the deck right through
the blazes. A lot of the most beautiful girls
come over from a battleship to skate with us."

The audience became interested. Old
Hughie and John Crasby looked at each other.

"Ain't he the damnedest liar outta hell?"
asked John.

Old Hughie shook his head as though it
were heavy with words.

"That's what beer does to a man," he commented at last.

"But anyway—" continued the soldier, "the
girls stayed with us. An admiral, about eighty-
eight years old, followed them and a sailor
knocked him off the ship with a book by Oscar
Wilde.

[177]

"There was an old Irishman on the ship waiting on the nigger admirals. Every time the niggers'd yell 'Come here Mick', the Irishman would cross himself.

"We were forty-nine thousand seven hundred and eighty-one and two-thirds miles from the coast of England, and seventy miles from Ireland. We could hear the Irish roll over in bed. We heard an old mick say, 'Thank ye Bridget!' And then he snored while Bridget got up.

"We hugged the girls tighter and laughed.

"But the admiral threw the Oscar Wilde book back on the deck and yelled—'The curse of a just God be on all ye devils.' He got his curse.

"The girls flew away quickly. You never saw anything lovelier. Water and the sun glistened on their legs and little cakes of ice dropped from their hearts."

The stranger looked dramatically at the ceiling and thundered:

"And as God in or out of His Heaven is my judge—we all got elephantisis. It started at our feet. They swelled till they stuck over the deck. We saw the admirals hugging the girls on the other ship and sailing away to the wars. Our ears became longer and wider than elephants.

" 'Lord have mercy' screamed the cook as he swelled out of the kitchen . . . 'When this thing comes up to our hearts we'll die.'

"The roar of the water melting off the ship was like the crashing roar of ten thousand Niagaras. The heat was so terrible it melted the smoke stack. The cold was so awful it froze the first mate's mouth shut. We grew so tall with the disease that our heads poked through the clouds and our shoulders shoved the stars out of place. It started to rain and the eagles flew down and stole our watches . . . pecked them right out of our pockets—as God is my judge. . . ."

The roving beer drinker looked at my grandfather.

Old Hughie became so excited with the tale that he dropped a quarter. The stranger picked it up and said to the bartender, "A glass of beer,

[179]

please," and then to Old Hughie, "Thank you, my good man."

He swallowed the beer. He smacked his lips.

"And believe it or not . . . the ship got the same disease. It began to swell over eighty miles of ocean each way.

" 'My God,' yells the captain. 'We'll have to shove this ship away from the coast of Ireland —we'll be grounded in the mud if we don't.' So we all waded in the ocean and put our shoulders to that ship. The captain stepped on a whale. You could hear it squish. 'Them damn worms. They always come out on the ground when it rains in this latitude.'

"The moon fell out of the sky and splashed water all over Ireland. A million geese bigger than ships swam over the sea and ate the moon up quick like a piece of yellow corn bread. Then the sun fell into the ocean and went out like a match in a bucket of water. A dippy dossis, that's a fish a thousand times larger than a whale, got its tail burned as the sun fell and it flew right against the ship and hit the captain in the eye.

"Suddenly there was no more light like me and you have seen. It turned green and blue. Then it faded and a pink-blue light came in over the sea. Dazzling angels colored like peacocks and more beautiful than the bubbles on beer, flew arm-in-arm together a million miles above us."

The stranger laughed as though something had caught in his throat.

"The second mate, like every sailor since oceans were made, had thoughts of women where his brain was supposed to be.

"He looked up at the angels and screamed, 'Oh—look—look—they're women and men angels—they're huggin' each other.'

"I looked up. They were ten thousand feet long. And believe me or not, gentlemen, their gigantic osculations shook the sky. Millions of little baby angels began to fly and sing—

" 'Down where the wurzburger flows—'

"The sky kept shaking till it fell into the sea. Another sky formed like new skin on a baby's

[181]

breast. It was the strangest thing you ever saw.

"I looked at the captain. His face was as scared and empty as my glass." The stranger frowned. . . .

"Bartender!!"

The mug was filled.

The beer disappeared as though it had been thrown into a funnel. "Suddenly the angels began to bray. They flew a few hundred thousand miles closer and I saw that their ears were longer than ours . . . they looked exactly like jackasses on wings—only they had no tails . . . they were eating shamrocks out of the meadows in the sky. Their wings went still and they all dropped right into Ireland." The stranger looked at Old Hughie. "And that's how the Irish came to the world."

Another roar of laughter followed.

Old Hughie, with a look of disgust, explained: "Indade it was not in Ireland they dropped—there's no jackasses in Ireland."

"No," returned the veteran quickly, "they've all come to America."

Old Hughie, like a proud man, ignored the thrust.

"It was in some brewery they dropped— where your father worked."

"Indeed not," retorted the stranger, "a jackass is not smart enough to light in a brewery— see there," the stranger pointed to a whisky advertisement on the wall—the picture of a mule heavily laden with whisky, "that proves what I say—I saw that mule falling in Ireland."

CHAPTER XIV

BULL RUN OF THE SOUL

My grandfather, anxious to turn the tide of battle, said to the stranger:

"I'll tell ye what I'll do. I'll dhrink two whiskies to aich mug o' beer ye dhrink—an' I'll put ye to slape under the brass railin' here."

The keen old Irishman knew that men in the crowd would furnish the drinks.

The whisky collector spoke up:

"All right—I'll bet on Hughie an' buy liquor for both."

The hero of Bull Run turned to Old Hughie and said:

"Stranger—why are you so rash . . . don't you know that my father was a brew-master in France for sixty years . . ."

"I don't give a damn if he was Quane Victoria's aunt—I'm goin' to dhrink ye unconscious as ye should be—a stranger comin' in to

[184]

groups o' gintlemen an' talkin' about yere damn wooden leg."

"Now it's glass for glass," said the bartender . . . "the man here'll be allowed two minutes more on each drink, Hughie—he's got more to drink."

"Who—me?" asked the one-legged man. "It's even, Stephen—as far as I'm concerned—minute for minute—glass for glass—I'll take no unfair advantage of a man. I learned chivalry at Bull Run—every man had a chance there—and they all took it."

"All right then. . . . I'll dhrink three glasses o' whisky to one of his beer—I'll taich him to brag."

"My wooden leg is hollow stranger—it holds a barrel."

"Oh—an' I don't give a flip o' the praist's cassock if it holds two barrels. If ye got a brain in yere talky head at all I'll make ye dhrunk."

The crowd stood close and laughed. Liquor was placed on the bar.

Old Hughie was steady as an iron rod.

[185]

The stranger reeled about the saloon. He raised a hand.

"All I ask now, gentlemen, is that you don't give the bout to my whisky drinking opponent —until you see me lie down and close my eyes for an hour. Was it not the Duke o' Wellington who yelled, 'Don't give up the ship,' I am of the breed—what would my grandfather, who was the greatest brewer of ale in Ireland, think of his son if he lost to a man like that? And if I lose I will do so like Attila the Hun at Valley Forge—who explained to Washington in the retreat from Bull Run—'The grass never grows where my horse's feet have slipped.' I am not a man who cries in his beer. I'll die fighting."

"Niver mind—dhrink yere beer—we'll make up our own lies," grunted my grandfather.

The word soon spread along Spring Street that Old Hughie Tully was trying to put a beer drinker "under the table." The saloon was soon filled. Men stood on chairs and watched the rivals.

[186]

"We're out of Three Star Hennessy, Hughie —will Old Taylor do?"

"Shure," replied Hughie—"I can bate this bum dhrinkin' if I dhrink rat poison."

"Well, that's what ye're drinkin', stranger," said the man, scraping his wooden leg on the floor.

John Crasby looked in a mug which the stranger placed on the bar. "There's another sup in there yet," he said, lifting the mug. "Drink it all—no fair leavin' any."

"I beg your pardon, gentlemen, that was an oversight—such mistakes are often made by the leading beer drinkers."

The saloon did a rushing business.

Everybody drank. The wine rooms and the back yard were filled with men. Many wagers were made. To Old Hughie's credit as a drinking citizen, he was a two to one favorite.

"But watch this other fellow," said a well-known German beer drinker from New Bremen, ten miles away. "He was in New Bremen last week. He put the four Hauser boys under the table in six hours."

[187]

The stranger with a mug in each hand, pounded his wooden leg on the floor and yelled—

"Remember what Newton said, gentlemen— give him a lever and he'd roll over the world— the same here, men—give me a big enough tank and I'll drain the breweries of Egypt. My father wasn't a brew-master in Germany seventy years for nothing."

Old Hughie, like a grim fighter, lost no motion. He seemed to feel that the least effort might tilt his brain into alcohol. On his face was the expression of a drowning man who tries to keep his chin above water.

His rival staggered about the saloon, talking loudly. He took the battered hat from his head.

"See the holes in this hat, gentlemen—shot through by whisky drinkers after I put 'em under the table."

Old Hughie made no direct comment.

"Kape yere eye on him," he said to John Crasby. "They're beginnin' to git licked whin they brag."

John Crasby watched the stranger. He examined each mug as it was placed upon the bar.

Hours passed. Still the men drank.

"Let's give them a recess," suggested the collector, "we'll be arrested for drownin' 'em— is it all right with you, Hughie—and you?" turning to the one-legged man.

Hughie conferred with John Crasby.

"Only fifteen minutes," said Old Hughie. . . . "I don't want to git outta the swing of the drink agin—my brain is in fine fettle now."

It was agreed to suspend liquid hostilities for a quarter of an hour.

The one-legged man stood with his back to the bar, arms outspread. "He'll be fallin' soon," said John Crasby to Hughie.

"I'm afraid not—the dhrunken scalawag— thir niver was sich a dhrinker since the night o' the big wind in Ireland."

Old Hughie scratched his head.

"But at any rate—whin I was a pidler in—"

"Gentlemen," shouted the one-legged man, "you have perhaps forgotten my original mission among you. I have come as a patriot home

[189]

from the wars—wounded—legless—but not dead—I come among you to obtain money with which to buy a new leg—this leg I now wear is worn and warped with the years. I was not an officer in the army, gentlemen—officers do not lose their legs in the cause of glory. I fought and died, gentlemen, that all men might be free to escape from the Bull Runs of the soul—my distinguished opponent here perhaps does not understand that emotion that kindles in the heart of the soldier—for did he not call my poem a lot of mush?"

"He'll talk himself under the table," Old Hughie whispered to John Crasby. "It's the talk that makes min dhrunk—it unsits their brain."

"Now whin I was a pidler—"

"And, gentlemen—hidden away as we are here from the stress and strife of daily life—I would fain say a word about how legs are lost—

"I too was a soldier in the army of love. I fought under the banner of the noblest young woman in Turkey. She was more beautiful than the wondrous maiden of whom our great

[190]

drinking companion, Lord Byron Burns, of other days wrote . . .

"Her overpowering beauty made me feel—
It would not be idolatry to kneel—

"She loved me as truly as a woman ever loved a man. And she was false. She entered the Sultan's harem against my wishes. She became the Sultan's favorite against her own.

"My old father came from the brewery in Kansas and pleaded with the Sultan. 'The boy has only one wife to give the Sultan—' my father said—'Please do not make her your favorite,' but it was all of no avail—at last I found the Sultan on the top of his building forty stories up—he was all alone—'Sult'—I said—'they will read in the papers to-morrow that you committed suicide. Even he who doubts will believe it—if he thinks of your fifty wives he will believe that you fell forty stories into the very arms of your women. It is a terrible vengeance I seek—caused by a terrible grief—but desire for women is the graveyard of greater men than yourself—you shall be

folded forever in the company of the greatest
men that ever lingered among us—"

"'Sir'—said the Sultan—'don't be a God
damn fool—you take your women seriously—
my business in life is women—a mere jump of
forty stories would not kill me—and if I am
not out of breath when I fall—I will hound
you with all the soldiers of civilized Europe and
the women-loving children of Ireland—I will
chase you over mountain and dale and pin you
to the walls of Jerusalem with the bullets of
my soldiers—' he shrugged his shoulders—
'What is a woman, however beautiful, to a man
like the Sultan,' he patted his chest, 'who can
get another—I would bid you be careful—
senorita—and besides—this woman you love so
devoutly—who is she—do you remember all
the roses in your walk through a garden—be
civilized, my friend—you were intelligent
enough to run from Bull Run—then why do
you show such crass stupidity here—ho—ho—
ho—ho—because you love a woman—go careful with murder my friend—you come from
more ignorant shores—there are no murders in

Turkey over women—wise men—we make them wear veils—their beauty is that which we men alone may see—in your countries—or at least it was when I traveled incognito over the realms of women with Edward the Seventh, then the beloved Prince of Wales—the beauty of women is for themselves—they preen before mirrors—and as they preen—in their minds comes the destruction of men—remember friend—men were free before mirrors were invented by a man who was insane—' "

"The time is up," shouted Old Hughie.

"Let him finish his tale. We must be courteous to the stranger within our gates," said the bartender, "besides, Hughie—have compassion —this man has loved a woman."

"Thank you—thank you profoundly," bowed the man with one leg—"you are a greater philosopher than most men who wipe bars—

"The Sultan weighed six hundred and six pounds. His body was gray and blue like rubber. But he was twenty feet tall so he did not seem so heavy.

" 'Women love a tall man,' he continued—

[193]

'if a tall man just remains quiet he will pass for Solomon with the smartest woman alive. The reason my realm is one of beauty and joy everlasting is because women do not think. They are told what to think in your nation— and what have you—more silly opinions—and less beauty.'

"He walked to a chart.

" 'When did your wife leave you?' he asked.

" 'Three months ago,' I replied.

" 'Then why this haste,' he thought seriously for some moments. 'It will be at least eleven months according to the most precise regulations of my women tabulators before I can even see her. Some very beautiful women have remained in my harem for as long as three years before they could even be admitted to my presence. Only four years ago I had to call in four kings from Christian Europe to help me give them audiences. So you see—sad man of love—that that which breaks your heart is but a dreary incident in the life of another man. All the troubles in the world, my sad man of love, are caused because men cannot lie still in

[194]

bed.' He turned swiftly from the chart.

" 'What were you doing in Turkey with your beautiful wife?'

" 'I was a missionary, Sire—and my wife worked with me in the saving of souls. Only three nights before she was captured for your harem she had saved forty of your heathen Turks. She was devout—and read her Bible each hour.'

"The Sultan raised his hand. 'It's no wonder she left—your Bible—I am told—does not bring peace to women. Only love can do that —and you denied it to her. No beautiful woman wishes to convert heathens. My long years as Sultan have taught me that. My men have searched the realms of the world for beautiful women. No beautiful woman was ever found among the lady missionaries. Saving souls is for ugly people with minds bitter as the thoughts of death. For what does it matter, my friend, how you walk to the grave—the test is always—what is important. Whether one be a scavenger of souls—or in love with a woman.' "

[195]

The stranger wept for a moment.

"But ah, she was lovely. Before we took ship for Turkey she converted a man in New York who said he was an alderman. She was alone with him in a room for several hours. And when they came out the man said he was saved. 'Much can be done with prayer,' the alderman said.

"She was being wrongfully detained by an evil woman in an evil house when I discovered her. After she, by the evil machinations of this evil woman, had stolen seven dollars from me I decided it was time to convert her and let her see the world.

"I used to teach women the way of virtue in such houses. It was a hard task.

"At last she consented to elope with me and save sinners if I gave her the seven dollars. And when we were married she told me of her sinful life. And, ah, gentlemen—she too had her Bull Run of the soul.

"I thought of her wrongs as I stood before the Sultan.

" 'Jump—' I yelled, pulling a big gun from my pocket.

"The Sultan jumped out of the window. I watched him land on the pavement below. I turned from the window and started to leave the room.

"The Sultan had bounced back and stood before me.

" 'I have thought it all over,' he said politely —'I shall not chase you from my dominions. You are free to wander where you will. But still you will be in prison. For well I know that the man who takes one woman seriously will never be free. I bid you good morning.' He pushed me out of his presence."

"What became of the wife?" asked the whisky collector.

Before the man could answer he collapsed.

"I knew it," smiled Old Hughie, "he talked himself under."

"Well he's just a travelin' bum," put in John Crasby.

"Indade, an' he's worse than that," returned my grandfather, "he's a beer drinker."

He rubbed his chin—

"Now whin I was a pidler in the South—"

[197]

CHAPTER XV

DITCH DIGGERS

In two weeks my father again came to St. Marys. He greeted me with no concern when he met me with my grandfather.

He had an old gray valise. It was shaped like a long box. Six heavy straps held it shut.

Empty bottles, corkscrews, a rusty beer can and several pipes were scattered about the room. An extra shirt, and an old necktie were in the bottom of a bureau drawer. He carried a very sharp razor with him. By some process known only to a near-sighted ditch digger, he managed to shave off every other whisker on his face.

Drunk or sober, he would shave each morning. When finished, his face resembled a red map of Ireland, dotted here and there with withered vegetation. He would lift his long red mustache and remove here and there the hair from the edge of his upper lip. This was no doubt done in order to give his mustache the proper swing downward. It gave him the appearance of a walrus.

My father contended with a group of ditch diggers in his room that desire for liquors always skipped a generation.

"How about you and Grandad?" I asked during a lull.

Father squinted at me with a puzzled smile. The ditch diggers laughed—

"The kid's all right, Jim—who'd o' thought o' that?"

A hunchback mud thrower slapped me on the shoulders hard enough to knock me forward. "You slipped one under your old man's belt that time."

The men laughed at my father.

"Well," he returned shaking the burning sensation of raw whisky from him, "a young fool can ask questions, a wise man can't answer."

My father always carried ten-cent paperbacked novels about with him.

Whether or not he had discrimination regarding their contents has always remained a mystery.

There were good and bad ditch-diggers

in his opinion. Books he did not discuss.

Such authors as Charles Garvice, Bertha M. Clay, Balzac, Dumas, Daudet, Scott, Cooper, Dickens, Hardy, Zola, Hugo and "The Duchess" made up part of his travelling library at different times.

He liked books about women. I first read "Sappho," "Camille," "Tess of the D'Urbervilles" and Flaubert's "Madame Bovary," in my father's paper-backed collection.

He once bought a collection of poetry in a paper cover.

He read a few lines and threw the book on the floor. He looked around for a drink. Finding none, he kicked the book under the bed and left the room.

I read all the books that father had. Among others were "Cousin Bette" and "The Hunchback of Notre Dame."

I remembered the names of the authors. My father gave me fifty cents to buy more books. I bought "Pere Goriot," "Paul and Virginia," "The Scarlet Letter," "Les Miserables," and "Germinal."

At no time in my life has such passion been given to anything.

Goriot and Jean Valjean haunted me for months. Enraptured, I told the tale of the French bread thief to my father. He listened quietly.

"I've read it," was all he said.

It was years before I could sense Hugo's falseness to life. I have not read him since.

The preface to "Paul and Virginia" told me that Napoleon had asked the author, "When are you going to give us another 'Paul and Virginia'?"

Zola made me mentally ill.

I took him too seriously.

Years later I discovered his romantic realism, and wondered why even as a child, he had fooled me.

My father read these books, and more, without comment.

He was busy with liquor and life. He may have felt that they were not worth discussion. I do not know. His comment on Pere Goriot's daughters was—

"Women are that way."

My sister came to the room on Sunday morning. Father sat near the window which faced Spring Street. He had a book in his hand and a bottle of whisky between his feet.

The church bells were ringing all over the town. Virginia looked about the room with sad eyes.

"I've come to take Jimmy to church," she said to my father.

Our parent rose and splashed tobacco juice into a spittoon.

"All right," he said indifferently, seating himself.

"But I don't want to go, Virginia—I went every morning for six years—that's enough," I said.

My sister looked pleadingly at my father.

He caught the look, lifted his bottle, shrugged his shoulders and said, "It's up to the kid," and took a long drink.

Virginia talked to me about my soul. She begged me with all the eloquence of seventeen.

My father paid no attention. Neither did I.
When she had finished I exclaimed—"I'll
never go again."

I never did.

She stood in the center of the room and
looked at me. She held a prayer book and
rosary in her hand.

"I'll say a prayer for you," she said sadly.

"Say one for me while you're at it," said my
father, rising and aiming at the spittoon again.

I could hear Virginia walking on the silent
street below.

My father looked up from his book.

"Why did ye not go?" he asked.

"*Because*," I replied.

He took a swig from the bottle and volunteered—

"It's as good as anything else."

My father outgrew many things. He remained a Democrat.

He was a passionate admirer of Grover
Cleveland. So was Grandad Tully.

I remember hearing them talk of an incident
in Cleveland's life. When it was learned that

[203]

Cleveland was the father of a bastard child, his friends and others were alarmed.

"What will we do about it?" they asked.

"Print it," replied Cleveland.

Old Hughie Tully took a silver dollar of my father's money which lay on the bar.

He spoke to the bartender, saying: "Here's some idle money—let's drink."

My grandfather was irate.

"The veery ideah—of any man peerin' into the great Cleveland's bizness wit' a woman," he became more angry. He hit the bar.

"The very nerve of it—why I'd vote for Cleveland now if he had more bastards than the King of Ingland."

"And the old boy likes his drink too," put in the bartender.

"Shure—an' why wouldn't he," exclaimed Old Hughie—he's a *MAN* . . . God love the big belly of him, an' the big brain—he's the bist dimmycrat of thim all."

To tease Old Hughie, a drinker at the bar chanted:

"The boat is coming around the bend,
Goodbye old Grover, goodbye—
'Tis loaded down with Harrison men—
Goodbye old Grover, goodbye."

Old Hughie drank feverishly and shouted—
"Do ye hear the words comin' outta the empty head—the wind's blowin' inside it—"

My father had given much thought to the wiles of women. He said to me a few months after I had left the orphanage, "They're all alike—some man can get 'em all."

We were in his bedroom above the pool room. Two bottles of "gunshot" whisky were near his pillow.

Save for a red flannel shirt, wide open, he was naked as truth.

I groped for his meaning.

His long arms, his rope-muscled legs, his immense chest were covered with hair.

"Your mother," he said, "would o' fell too—they're all alike."

He was restless that Sunday night. The saloons were closed.

[205]

He interspersed talk with the rattling of liquor down a heavy throat.

He never followed a drink of whisky with water.   He mixed nothing with raw liquor.

"No use spoilin' it," he said often.

Late into the night he told me of what he had learned about life and women.

Early next morning his ditch-digging friends called on him.

"This your youngest boy, Jim?" one of them asked.

"Sure," said my father indifferently.

The delvers into mud felt my arms and shoulders.

They laughed heartily.

"He's a husky kid."

"Ain't you gonna buy a drink, Jim?"

"Sure thing," replied my father.

He reached into a bureau drawer for a rusty tin bucket.   He took a bacon rind and greased the bottom and sides.

"That's the stuff," said one of my father's friends.   "It'll make the beer fall flat and stick like lead—we'll git twice as much."

[206]

"An' sure—don't I know it," retorted my father.

"Here son," he said, "Go down to Oland's on the corner and tell 'em your dad sent ye for a can of beer—twenty cents' worth."

I took the bucket and two dimes.

I asked the bartender for a dime's worth of beer.

I watched him hold the bucket as far from the brass faucet as possible to make more foam in the bucket.

Before returning to my father I put water in the beer.

The men drank with wry faces. "It's damned weak," they agreed.

My father sent another ditch digger after the next bucket of beer.

Later in the day he said to me, "Kid—never spoil a bucket o' beer for a nickel or a dime."

He frowned.

"I once knew of an Irishman who drank water—his stomick got rusty an' he died. But he niver mixed it with beer."

There was in my father but one touch of ego.

[207]

When drunk, which was often as convenience and chance would allow, he would bet money that he could throw a shovelful of dirt further than any man in Ohio.

And once, at an Irish picnic, he included the whole world.

A rival ditch digger heard him announce his claim to fame. He was from a German settlement at the other end of Auglaize County.

"You couldn't throw dirt over a Protestant's grave," he shouted.

The saloon was full of men and the odor of frying fish. Above the noise could be heard the bragging of the rival diggers of ditches. It ended with both men placing a bet of ten dollars each in the hands of John Crasby and my grandfather's bosom friend.

A site was selected where a large creek was being dug with the aid of horses and scrapers. My father rode with the German. Two drunken generals surveying a muddy country could not have looked more important. A score of men followed. Shovels were procured. As both men were right-handed it was decided to throw the dirt on the right side of the creek. Two men were to mark the spot where the largest portion of the dirt landed.

It was a drizzly day.

Each man was allowed ten minutes' practice. The German stood in the bottom of the creek, the banks of which were far above his head. He threw the dirt with such speed that it hummed through the air. My father merely threw the dirt a short distance.

When the time was up each man stripped for action.

They stood, bare to the waist, in the drizzling weather.

Gum boots reached to their hips. There was shouting and laughter from the men on the bank.

When it was discovered that my father had beaten the German by three feet, the rival ditchers returned arm-in-arm to the saloon.

John Crasby, the holder of stakes, was nowhere to be found. He was at last discovered with Old Hughie in the Horseshoe Saloon.

They had spent the money for drink.

[209]

CHAPTER XVI

THE MERMAID AND THE WHALE

WITH his valise across his back, peddler fashion, my father walked away.

Our parting was casual.

My loneliness **was** intense, my heart bitter. I said no word.

My father left me his small library of paper-backed novels. I was working in a combination saloon and restaurant.

I stood in back of the lunch counter, sleeves rolled to my elbows, a greasy apron tied about me. The dish sink was so near the street that people could see me as they passed.

There soon took root in my heart the false weed of humility, which often conquered pride.

It was apparent to the rustic drunkards and glib salesmen, who teased me as a result.

The owner of the restaurant joined in the merriment with his customers.

The teasing made life weigh more heavily upon me. I was often ashamed to go on the street when the day's work had ended. Instead, I would go to my little room and read—with my world in upheaval.

One evening a young farmer who did not like the Lawlers became personal.

When my grandfather came, I threw my childish pride away and broke down in his arms. He caressed me roughly, and said—

"Take yere own part, me boy—if ye let thim kick ye at yere age—ye'll niver do nothin' but crawl the rist o' yere life."

His words made me brave.

"Come fer a long walk wit' me," he beseeched, "It'll be undher the moon on the dark streets, an' no one will see an old man an' his boy."

As if to ease my heart, he talked constantly.

"You shouldn't be washin' daishes. Yere too wild a bird for so greasy a cage—"

"We're both savages me boy—did ye iver think of that—well no—yere too young—but it's much I know of Ireland an' her payple—

[211]

you an' me come out of mud huts—our payple were dumber than the hogs they killed for the praist—indade, an' I know—we are the *Red* Irish—wit' the angry eyes an' the bleuit faces.

"We were little more than two-legged cattle held together by the Holy Mither Church— a hundred years ago—we're Danes an' Irish, me boy—the descindents of big red Danes who traveled the says in canoes—an' who came into Ireland an' had their way wit' the lovely girls —a kind fate for a Dane—"

The old man stumbled at the curb. "Why in the hill ye have to stip up an' down like a horse is more than I know in this town—they git enough money outta the saloons to have dacent straits."

He recovered his equilibrium when he saw me smile.

"Laugh at yere old grandad an' he'll till ye *no* more about Ireland."

"I'm sorry, Grandad," I said quickly. "Please go on."

"There's nothing to go on to now, me boy, excipt to tell ye to niver trust a woman an' walk on yere heels round the dead—yere old Grandaddy knows things. He kin lie in bed at night an' hear the world go round.

"He's walked over many a ragin' strame on the rocks—an' his fayt have bin wet wit' the blood of life—an' that's made me catch the cold of wisdom—an' helps me to rade min's hearts behind their faces—thire's somethin' in ye an' yere brither Tom—so maybe ye'll both git hung—for that's the way of rale Irish— they git throttled in their slape—so that's why I talk to ye—I'd give a quart of Peoria licker to be able to watch ye from my grave. I'd shove the clouds in Satan's eyes foriver if I could see ye twenty years from now. I'd go an' git yere mither out of her grave in Glynwood— an' I'd say to her—

" 'Look Biddy—look—that's our boy—him that is of yere blood an' mine—an' the great sad heart of ye'—and Biddy would weep for joy—while the wind blew through the fire of her hair—an' the grand proud form of her stood straight up.

" 'See Biddy Lawler,' I'd say, 'For him did

we drame not in vain—he's our boy wit' the
hurt hearts of us undernathe his own—he's a
little mad Biddy—bein' a Lawler.' I'd say
very quiet like—'but ye can't have iverything
Biddy—and if he's a great son—well Biddy—
quit yere cryin'—or I'll send ye back to yere
grave. I'm takin' ye for a walk, Biddy, to
watch yere son that's the son of my son—don't
ye see, Biddy—can't ye see. He's the great
Goovenor of Ohio—an' he learned his politics
from his old Grandad—an' how to carry his
licker—an' from you Biddy he got—iverything
that's in April—the quick tear an' the pity for
fool that nade not be'—thin whin ye'd gone
I'd go galavantin' over the blue meadows wit'
Biddy—an' out of their graves would come the
mithers of min—an' thim that died with the
birth of their children would be first—an' all
of thim would sing softer than the fithers of
robins in May—while Biddy and I played
marbles with the stars."

He laid his shovel-twisted hand upon my
shoulder.

"I talk like a woman, me boy—I'm an old

mick wit' a drame that broke in his head—"

He touched his temple.

"There's a lot ye'll learn, me boy, as the years pass. None of it'll be worth much. Ye'll break yere heart in yere own way in the ind. I kin tell by the way ye look at me that ye were born to suffer. Yere mither was like that.

"But don't take it so hard—I'm no happier than ye are, boy—an' niver have I been—if it wasn't for whisky I'd drink bluin' in Holy Water to kape from goin' crazy. They think I don't think because I'm an old man with fire in his throat—but whin I'm sausage for the worms, me boy—I want ye to remimber—that Old Hughie Tully was not a fool."

A faint moon poured dotted shadows through the arched maple trees.

The old man walked slowly and ponderously. The heavy nails in his shoes scratched the cement pavement.

We passed under an arc light.

My grandfather's face was a hard mask with soft eyes.

[215]

The light faded behind us. Even the moon was hidden.

"Ah well—ah well—I should o' stayed a pidler in the South—I don't belong here—an' I niver have—I belong where the hearts are warmer—where the women's voices are softer —an' the moon shines aven in the daytime."

We walked some distance in silence. As if to relieve congested lungs, the old man blew a deep breath.

"Indade—I'd give a million o' the Lord's gold if I were yere age—I'd lave here with the robins—a-rollin' stone may gather no moss— but a rovin' dog sometimes picks up a bone— an' that's what makes min happy—the sudden things—the wimmen a pidler sees,—but not for too long—the biggest bottle gits empty in the ind—an' thin ye kin whistle with it.

"For it's niver the woman ye can trust too long, me boy.

"A friend of mine was a bold bad man in Ireland. He killed so many Inglish it broke the good Quane's heart. Indade he hated the

whole world an' trusted nobody but his sweet-
heart. She betrayed him."

He held a sardonic laugh in his throat.

"Why I aven knew a mermaid who wint back
on her vow of holy matrimony. She took the
ring off her tail an' scampered away.

"She'd come up for air one time when
Johnny Dodagen saw her—an' bein' Irish an'
a fool—he fell in love. She was so beautiful
the waves turned gold where she'd swim—an'
thin they'd turn into waves of rainbows.

"Well, Johnny married her with an old blind
praist. He sat by the bed an' covered her tail
—the praist he thought the lady was ill—"

The old man laughed—

"Ye know—or maybe ye don't—mermaids
have babies faster than aven poor payple—
about six a month if they go to confession; an'
if they don't it's a dozen a month. In three
months there were thirty nice little Dodagens
—an' they all had Irish faces an' fishes tails—"

"Johnny wanted her to go to confession and
she would not—and woe an' behold one Sunday
morning she took her thirty nice little Doda-

gens an' wint to the say—an' niver came back to him. Johnny Dodagen came near to faintin' ivery time a shark's tail flapped in the water— he thought it was his dear wife or the oldest girl—but it was no use—the Dooblin papers reported she'd married a whale an' wint to live in London.

"One of the Dodagen boys grew up to be a lawyer—an' he was the bist in Ingland—he was—a strange family was the Dodagens."

CHAPTER XVII

THE BEST DRESSED MAN IN ST. MARYS

WE turned to the left off Spruce Street.

A row of dilapidated saloons faced the railroad.

"We'll go in here," Grandfather suggested in front of a saloon, "and rist a while. I don't want the damned rheumatiz twitchin' at the heart o' me."

He laid a quarter on the table as we seated ourselves.

A man entered.

"Hello Hughie," he said quickly to my grandfather.

"Why hello Jack," my grandfather greeted the man.

Old Hughie seemed highly honored. Jack Cullen was one of the leading lawyers in that part of Ohio, and district attorney for Auglaize County. His eyes were snapping black, his face strong. His hair was sleek and combed backward in black waves. Gold nose-glasses added much to his appearance in my boyish mind. Known as "the best dressed man in St. Marys," he patronized no local tailor. His clothes were made in Columbus, the capital of Ohio, ninety miles away. It was said that the man who made his suits had been "President McKinley's tailor."

I had often seen him pass through the restaurant on the way to the saloon. He seemed a being from another world so wealthy and well-dressed. After watching him, I more deeply regretted my job as a washer of dishes.

"Have a drink, Hughie," he asked cordially.

"Indade and I will, Jack," chuckled my grandfather, starting to rise.

"Sit still, Hughie—I'll sit with you."

The bartender brought a bottle of whisky.

"Three Star Hinnissy," laughed Old Hughie. And Jack Cullen said:

"Remember the time, Hughie, you got drunk on that brand."

"Which time was that?" asked Old Hughie —Then smacking his lips,

"Ga-wd—that's a drink for the Prisidint."

"It's none too good for you, Hughie," responded the lawyer.

"The Lord bless ye—ye know how to plaze an old man—I said to yere father long ago, I did—Jack'll be the goovernor of the state— he will—if the great heart in him don't shake the brains out of his head."

The lawyer looked keenly at my grandfather.

"Hughie," he said, "you should have been a politician."

Old Hughie poured another drink.

"Not with you in the same state, Jack."

"Thanks, Hughie. There would be room for us both." The lawyer turned:

"Is this your grandson, Hughie?"

"Yes—it's Jim's boy."

Then, as if anxious to change the subject Old Hughie said quickly—

"Jack—I heard a good story to-day—The praist tried to git a man to confiss—'Is there nothin' more ye kin tell,' says he—'Not even the slightest thing,'—

"The man thought a long time.

" 'Oh I did kill a lawyer,' he says, 'I nearly forgot.'

" 'An' why didn't ye tell me sooner—' asked the praist—'I'd o' give ye absolution right away.' "

Jack Cullen smiled.

"There'd be no need of lawyers, Hughie, if people kept out of trouble."

He looked at me for some seconds. And put his hand on my shoulder.

"How long were you in the orphanage, son?" His words were an embrace.

"Six years."

Cullen looked at my grandfather.

"Has Biddy been dead that long?"

Grandfather nodded his head.

"She was a fine woman," said the lawyer.

"The bist of the Lawlers," put in my grandfather.

There were at least thirty votes in the Lawler tribe.

Jack Cullen made no comment.

There was a moment's pause.

Old Hughie's face was alive. The lawyer

wiped his gold nose-glasses. He looked at me.

"Well—you'll come through all right. People either do or they don't," he said with some finality. He swallowed twice, and tried to adjust a silk scarf which was already in correct position.

He rose quickly.

"I'd like to talk to you some time, my boy— come up to my office—will you?" He spoke a word to the bartender on his way out of the saloon.

I was too confused to answer.

The bartender said to me as we left, "Mr. Cullen left this for you." It was a five dollar bill.

"I'll take care of it for ye," volunteered my grandfather. He still has it.

We walked down Spring Street in the direction of the cottage in which grandfather lived.

Across the street, on the second floor, was the lawyer's office. It was still well lighted.

The largest window in the town stretched across it. In a half circle above were the names

[223]

of the lawyer's Irish partner and himself. Beneath were the words—"Attorneys at Law."

The next day Jack Cullen stopped at the lunch counter and chatted with me a few moments.

He became the one man above the station of a laborer in St. Marys who talked to me without ridicule.

Like most men, he was unhappily married.

The daughter of a factory superintendent fell in love with him. She was very beautiful. Her form was perfect, her eyes dark brown, her hair long, wavy, and dark. She was graceful as a gull in the wind, and clean and trim like a hound ready for the running.

Jack Cullen was said to have been in love with her.

His wife sued for a divorce.

The beautiful girl was named.

The lawyer left town.

The divorce was granted.

The girl was said to have died by choking to death upon the core of an apple.

She was pitied by all.

All of what happened to the lawyer, no man knows.

He too became a washer of dishes on a Lake Erie steamer. Next—he begged money with a tin cup on the streets of Cleveland.

*   *   *   *   *   *   *

Charles Mooney, a United States congressman from a Cleveland district, was from St. Marys.

The one time brilliant lawyer called upon Mooney. Derelict and dirty, he stood in the congressman's office. Hands trembling, emaciated, half blind, the once sleek black hair was now a ghoulish gray.

His head shook from side to side.

The winner looked at the loser.

Not recognizing Cullen, Mooney asked, "Is there something I can do?"

"Not much," replied O'Brien, "it's beyond all doing—" He assumed the posture of a young lawyer before a judge—with a half smile on his vagabond lips.

[225]

"But, Charlie—I'm glad for you—don't you remember Jack Cullen?"

The force of the man's identity overwhelmed Mooney. With quick intuition he walked toward his caller.

"Jack Cullen—I'm glad you're here."

"Glad I'm here, are you, Charlie—in my rags and my dirt—and my heart that's broken and dead, going drunken to my death."

The congressman put an arm around Cullen.

"Yes Jack—I'm *damned* glad you're here."

Like many sensitive men, Cullen hid defeat with a semblance of defiance.

His battered and dissipated face became transfused with scorn. He laughed shrilly.

The congressman handled the situation carefully.

Cullen was treated as though he were a successful lawyer who had lost his first case.

Mooney advanced him one hundred dollars, and bought him a suit of clothes.

He telephoned Cullen's former wife, and persuaded her to remarry him and begin life over.

She consented.

Jack Cullen left for the train.   The woman waited.

He never arrived.

He was later found in a Cleveland gutter; ragged, dead.

CHAPTER XVIII

THE MAD IRISH

AFTER twenty-eight years my uncle Dennis wrote to his brothers. It was the first word from him since the memorable spring in which my mother and her parents died.

A broken-down hotel porter in Oklahoma, he needed help.

His brothers were hard as only sentimental men can be.

They refused.

He was heard of no more.

Aunt Moll, bediamonded, and wealthy, grew more in favor with the brothers as the years passed.

When she died, all the brothers stood at her grave except the ex-horse thief and the man who had rescued her from the Methodist Church.

All were now on the last knoll of life, but in each heart the hot fire of drama still burned.

Tearless they stood, looking at each other, across the grave of a one time beautiful Lawler.

[228]

A final prayer for the departed died away. The expensive coffin was lowered.

"She's with Biddy now," said an uncle.

"Not with Biddy," returned Virginia.

All became quiet, with dramatic suddenness. Tom Lawler screamed.

"My God, Moll—"

It startled the birds in the trees.

A shovelful of earth rattled on the coffin.

Gossip in Ohio said that my favorite uncle, whom I always liked because he was a constant source of amusement to me, in a fit of anger against his family, drove to the poor house in an expensive automobile.

He was refused admittance.

At the time of mother's death, he loaned my father two silver dollars. My father, being more practical than sentimental, used them to keep her eyes closed. Tom Lawler considered this an insult. As a consequence he did not speak to my father for twenty-five years. "I gave him the money for grub—and not to close Biddy's dead eyes," was Tom Lawler's comment.

This man was literally a brother to tornado. He was tall, heavily-built, with a trim black mustache, Van Dyke beard, debonair, and lithe of movement, his voice musical and soft. He it was who married the daughter of the German land owner and restored the farm to the Lawlers'. Aunt Lode was gentle, patient, kindly. She loved my mother as a sister and we, children of destitution, were always treated with living consideration by her. Her eyes were always sad, she spent each day with chickens, ducks and animals on the farm.

Where he learned about wool I do not know. He was for sixteen years superintendent of a woolen mill in St. Marys. He had the blarney of an Irishman and save in anger, the soft manner of a parish priest. Anger transformed him immediately into the most tyrannical and ruthless of men.

In a rage over a trifle he once walked across his barnyard. He carried a pitch fork in his hand. A cow mooed within ten feet of him. This angered him the more. He chased the unfortunate creature with his pitchfork, "I'll teach you to moo at me—you damn four legged fool—"

The horrified cow escaped into the field.

*   *   *   *   *   *   *

My mother left fourteen dollars each to her six children.

One of her brothers borrowed the money. He returned it without interest, after we, in turn became of age and protested vigorously.

Even when a dollar would have appeased our hunger for several days, he made no mention of the money.

He was my father's favorite among the Lawlers.

A red-headed arrogant fellow, with heavy shoulders and heavier hands, his life was a long snarl.

On the day I became twenty-one, after seven years as a hobo, I returned to St. Marys for my fourteen dollars. Years later it occurred to me that I had tramped more than a thousand miles and had endured all the hardships of the road—to claim my small inheritance.

Full of whisky and venom I entered the saloon where stood my uncle.

He too was full of liquor and hatred toward me because I was "a disgrace to the family."

He frowned at me.

Feeling that one could never bluff a Lawler, I stood before him prepared to fight.

"I want fourteen dollars, Pete—*now!*" I said composedly. He was capable of holding his own with any roughneck in the world. His eyes threw terrible blows at me.

Prepared to dodge either fist, I stood firm.

Every one in the saloon was expectant.

Feet scraped on the floor. The atmosphere was tense.

An intuitive master of dramatic situations, his crooked mouth broke into a smile.

He put a long muscular arm about me.

"Sure Jim—I've got it all ready for you." He took a rubber band from a roll of bills and peeled off fourteen dollars.

"Hey men, this is my dead sister Biddy's boy —this is his birthday—Let's all drink." He treated the house twice.

We made merriment that night together. I
spent the fourteen dollars.

We never spoke to each other afterward.

CHAPTER XIX

GOOD-BYE, NELLIE!

THE Illinois authorities learned too late of John Lawler's release from the Ohio Penitentiary.

He arrived in a Canadian town on a windy wintry day. He had with him an old valise and twenty dollars. He secured work as a coachman. He literally lived with the handsome team which pulled the banker's carriage.

The citizens asked no questions of the man who loved horses.

No one knows just why he went so deftly and surely to a particular town.

It may have been that he carried a message.

A wealthy family perhaps learned that their son had died—a missionary in China—instead of a gallows-birds in Ohio.

It is all mysterious—except:

John Lawler was a trusty in the penitentiary the year Blinky Morgan was hung.

Morgan was even more silent than my uncle. The people of Ohio strangled him without ever

[234]

learning where he was from, or his real name.

These things have been mysteries for forty years.

He was a sombre, slow moving, quick-thinking Gael.

Morgan had some connection with people in Canada. He was on his way to that country when arrested for murder committed in Ohio.

Any confidence Morgan may have placed in my uncle during the ten months he awaited execution was never violated.

A fur store was robbed in Cleveland.

A week later two detectives went to Pittsburgh in search of the robbers. A suspect was arrested.

The officers started for Cleveland with him.

Several other men boarded the train about fifty miles from the Ohio city.

The detectives, their prisoner handcuffed between them, stared out of the window.

The men entered the car.

An iron coupling pin, wrapped in newspaper, crumpled one detective to the floor, brokenskulled, dead.

The men drew revolvers. The other detective escaped, screaming.

Three men, Morgan among them, were captured some weeks later while attempting to flee to Canada. Morgan had an alibi. It did not save him.

He was sentenced to hang.

The governor of Ohio, Joseph Benson Foraker, later to die in disgrace as a political grafter, refused to give him the benefit of the doubt, by commuting his sentence to life imprisonment.

Morgan had regular features. He was about forty years of age. His manner was that of a clergyman.

One of his eyes had been injured. He was called Blinky.

He wore glasses to hide the defect in his eye. His clothing was always dark. His scarf was either severe white or black.

He was polished, suave, debonair.

The prison guards became fond of him. They doubted his guilt.

He read everything possible. He would discuss all subjects but his own case—and religion. Unlike most Christians who are hung, he did not acknowledge God.

As he did not wish the news reporters to garble any verbal statement after his death, he wrote one to the warden. "There will doubtless be people who will not hesitate to declare that I died with a falsehood on my lips, simply because my assertions cannot correspond with their beliefs and prejudices . . . I am being judicially murdered to satisfy the clamor for a victim."

At his request only the visitors he invited were allowed to see him hang.

At five in the evening he ate dinner. He lay on his iron cot in the death chamber until eleven that night and stared at the ceiling. What his thoughts were—no one knew. Two hours before dying he rose and wrote letters.

At one that night the warden appeared with the death warrant.

The man about to die asked if the rope was ready. The official nodded. Morgan rubbed

[237]

his neck, and said, "This is an awful business, Warden."

He arrayed himself with precise care. He pinned roses and heliotrope in the lapel of his coat.

The march to the gallows began at 1:17.

A minute later the scaffold door suddenly opened. Morgan stood before the invited assemblage with the warden and two other official murderers.

While the rope was being adjusted a friend made some disturbance. He was ejected. Upon Morgan's request he was re-admitted.

Morgan looked around the room of death as the warden read the death warrant.

The doomed man sobbed several times, as the sentence was read. His glasses were wet with tears.

The black cap was adjusted. The officers stepped quickly from the vicinity of the trap.

Morgan dropped into eternity with two words on his lips. His throat rattled as though he would repeat them. He never did.

They were: *Good-bye, Nellie!*"

CHAPTER XX

A BANKER IN CANADA

JOHN LAWLER'S relatives never divulged his whereabouts, even the children were fiercely silent concerning him.

A man of iron, his spirit was not crushed by thirteen years in one of the most terrible of American jails.

Stronger than a cable of steel was his will. It never snapped. Unyielding to the end, he became a sardonic red and gray old man.

A close cropped mustache and beard hid the strong, tight, brutal mouth.

His eyes were ever those of a haunted man.

It was said of John Lawler in his younger days that all who knew him for an hour regretted it a lifetime. This may have been true. It could not have been said of his later years.

Cold, diffident, with a musical voice and a slight brogue, he went quietly down the long hill of life with the poise of a Chinese mandarin. In thirty-eight years he never left the town. He lived in the same house for thirty-four years. He would say no word for hours at a time. Several of us visited him. We were welcome always.

Like my mother, the ex-horse thief never knew how to laugh. Humor had early been strangled in his throat.

He married a banker's daughter. Her name was said to be Nellie. He died—owning the bank.

His identity was never questioned. The brigand easily became the gentleman of finance.

His daughters, educated at exclusive colleges, were not aware that their father was a convicted horse thief.

After being convicted his father said to him —"Did ye have no mercy on the team ye burned?"

Always inscrutable, the young man looked at his father with the expression of one too tired to answer the question of a child.

There was something in his favor. He had

none of the insincerity which makes possible all social intercourse.

The hauteur of his mien gained the respect and fear of lesser and luckier men.

When father, mother, sister and brothers wept over his conduct, he remained calm until they had regained control.

Many women loved him. With the exception of his wife and two daughters—he betrayed them all.

Married at forty, after a long prison term, he was either too tired or indifferent to interest himself further in women.

He was never known to have responded to a human emotion.

"One may as well kiss a block of ice," my mother once said of him.

But neither did he ever say an unkind word to the three women who clung to him until he was a very old man. The cold blood congealed in his heart at last. Like his father, he died of heart failure.

His house was large and white, with green

shutters. It was shielded from the road by immense trees and shrubs.

A weather vane—the bronze figure of a running horse, was on the front gable of his barn.

Two iron horses were used as hitching posts in front of his house.

Large iron negro jockeys stood at the sides of the horses. Their right arms were extended as if to grasp the lines. A joyful expression of welcome was upon their faces.

Schoolboys on a Hallowe'en prank, stole one of the horses.

The banker's wife was irate when it was discovered next day along a country road.

As a future precaution the banker had the iron horses imbedded in concrete.

He divided his time between his house and his vast ranch.

He seldom left his home at night.

During long winter evenings he would sit in his immense living room, while his wife and daughters made gay the house.

His girls studied music, and he developed ap-

preciation for the more thunderous rhythms of
the masters.

When they tried to tell him something of
Wagner's life, he would turn to "The Breeder's
Journal."

His mania for horses never left him. It in-
creased with age. His hands were always firm
on lines or bridle.

He could detect the least blemish on a horse.
He would stand at its head, his eyes oblique, his
face stern. Thumb and forefinger would lift
the horse's upper lip. He would look at its
teeth and tell the horse's age instantly. His
stern presence could control the mood of a stallion.

His ranch was stocked with many breeds of
horses.

He would seldom accompany his family on
Sunday.

That day he spent in the country. Horses
whinnied when he drew near.

No horse on his ranch was ever traded or
sold. A veterinary surgeon inspected them each
month. An animal had once broken a leg and

torn a hoof loose. The ex-horse thief was three weeks in deciding to have it shot. After it was put out of its misery, he remained away from the ranch for over a week.

He once bred an Arabian mare to a Percheron stallion. The offspring was fire and docility.

Though he had no use for it as a stallion, he would not have it neutered.

For some reason it appealed to him more than the other horses.

His youngest daughter named it Ali Baba. He called it Babe.

With the ex-horse thief and banker on his back Ali Baba would lift his knees high and prance down the road. He would keep the same pace for hours; his dark red body a gracefull mass of muscle beneath his somber burden.

He had a passion for feeding apples to horses. A boy would follow him each Sunday with a basket full of the luscious fruit. By deft manipulation he would insert the apple in the horse's mouth. The horses would neigh and trot across the meadow. One apple, and a pat on the nose was each animal's portion.

[244]

He never lost his carved-granite appearance. Age merely accentuated the hard fiber of his body. His step was ever elastic—and firm.

He was always reluctant to ride in an automobile. He never learned to drive. Only on rare occasions would he accompany his family in a machine. At such times he would remain in the rear seat and gaze at the passing landscape as he had on the way to the penitentiary.

Once in a while he would ride with his youngest daughter in her roadster. He would remain deep in thought while she dashed, hair blowing, cheeks red as fire, over the countryside.

The other Lawlers perpetually spouted the smoke of life. He was ever a furnace in which the fire had either gone out, or was under control.

With increasing age he became more aloof, even snobbish, as though people were not worth the bother.

The foundation of his wife's fortune had been built while he was stealing horses. It grew in value with the years. He merely allowed it to grow.

Silent, with an immense head, a Roman nose, a thin-lipped firm mouth and heavy chin, there grew up about him a legend. He was considered a wizard of finance.

He would sit at his heavy desk in a heavy chair. His very presence filled with awe the little unimaginative men who dabbled in figures.

He delighted in having his daughters' girl friends at the house.

For hours he would play checkers, or solitaire with cards. One after another the girls would try to vanquish him at checkers. He would sit, calm as Buddha, his strong mind concentrated on the game until he had won.

Roars of girlish laughter would follow each victory.

One winter night when a chinook wind drove across the avalanche of snow that was Saskatchewan, John Lawler's daughter read aloud to him the story of a western lynching.

Several girls were at the house. A game of checkers had been finished.

The banker gazed at the blazing logs in the fire.

. . . . A man served a year in jail for stealing a horse. When released he was threatened with death if he repeated the offense. Arrested for stealing another horse, he was found hanging from a limb next morning, his head tilted sideways—arms and legs stiff. A placard was fastened to the bosom of his shirt. On it were the words: "We gave him a chance to live—but he committed suicide."

"What a terrible story," said the banker's wife—"isn't there enough misery in the world without reading such things aloud, Patsy?"

The banker rose and placed another small log on the fire.

"Play something, Patsy dear," said her mother.

The girl's delicate hands thrummed the piano keys.

The one time horse thief looked at the fire and listened to the music.

When the others had gone to bed, John Lawler picked up the newspaper.

The chinook wind rattled the windows and doors.

Slowly he read again the story of the horse thief who was lynched.

CHAPTER XXI

BROTHERS AND SISTERS

THE years passed in dramatic parade. Virginia had always wanted to bring her mother's stray brood together. In a desperate fight against hunger, my brother Tom left for the Philippine Islands with the United States Army. Hardly seventeen years of age, he told the recruiting officers that he was twenty-one.

The rest of us were in St. Marys.

Another sister was too young to work.

The Ohio winter settled, dreary and monotonous. We lived in two rooms over a grocery store. Virginia was too tired after work to keep house. Anna was too young.

Virginia painted a glowing picture of the house we would at last have together. Children with hearts ignorant of homes listened intently. Two rusty second hand bed springs were stretched across pine boxes. A thin black curtain was between. A conglomerate collection of worn cooking utensils and chipped dishes were given by relatives.

We lived together like jackals seeking shelter from the cold. There was between us none of the polite deferences which make human propinquity bearable. Virginia was kindly always. Everything pressed upon her. Now she, who had never been known to spend a dime wisely, tried to run a household into which little money came. Alone in the miserable group was she unselfish. Alone was she worthy of the strong peasants who had preceded us.

Never during the long winter was there an hour's peace in the makeshift home.

I went to my work each morning at five. Through snow and mud and rain I would trudge two miles to the chain shop in order to prepare the fire for the chainmaker. The cold bit my sparsely clad body and filled my heart with venom against life. After an hour's work upon the forge the heat would be turned on in the shop. The working hours were pleasant—and warm. I often dreaded it when the day's work had ended.

Only people who were more miserable than ourselves came to our flat.

On Sundays, when the saloons were closed, I would often read a paper backed novel. Whenever a travelling theatrical company came to the town I would climb up the fire escape, pry open the window and sneak into the gallery.

Hunger and squalor were more easily endured than the loneliness of a groping boyhood.

With never a dollar to spend in a month, I would nightly wander in and out of saloons and recite doggerel, tell stories or trade anything possible for drinks. I acquired then a habit which has never left me. I learned to read faces by watching them reflected in the mirror in front of the bar. Thus, I learned never to look directly in a person's eyes. With people, it has helped me greatly. They always reveal themselves when not conscious of being watched.

All I know of human nature was learned in a saloon before I was twenty. I learned to dis-

[251]

tinguish between a laugh from the head and one from the heart. I gauged sincerity by the intonations of speech. I caught boredom with the lift of an eyelash at the bar. I have since found that men and women in far places of the world and in different social strata are fundamentally the same as those I first met in my formative years.

My oldest brother slept, when he worked, in a livery stable.

Each morning he brought the odor of horses with him to the breakfast table. Being the elder, and dogmatic Irish, he soon made laws for the family. The rest of the children, being of the same breed, resented his laws. With the exception of Virginia, it was a snarling household.

Every two weeks I was paid by the chainmaker for whom I toiled. A drunkard, he often lost several days' work during this period. As I only made a dollar in the two weeks, it went for board and lodging. As a result, Virginia often gave me twenty-five cents to spend at the end of my two weeks' labor.

[252]

My work with this chainmaker lasted several months.

Exasperated at the enforced idleness and loss of wages which his drinking entailed, I wrote with chalk upon the link room door:

"When old Ed Ryan's dead and in his grave—
No more bad licker will he crave—
But on his tombstone will be wrote—
'Many a bottle's gone down my throat.'"

Chainmakers and link heaters read the ungrammatical doggerel with laughter.

Ryan discharged me.

It was an occasion for a strike on the part of the link heaters. With sooty faces and tattered clothes, each boy left the fire at which he worked.

Ryan refused to allow me to work for him further.

The strike was settled when another chainmaker "traded boys" with Ryan. My new employer kindly gave me three dollars regularly every week. During the rest of the winter

[253]

I had a little money of my own to spend.

My oldest brother and Virginia fought over the bills which steadily mounted higher. There was never quite enough money between us to pay for rent and food.

We had neither enough heat nor bed clothing. Between extreme poverty and jangled nerves our home became a nightmare. The saloon was my escape from its sordid atmosphere.

I would loiter at different bars until midnight. I often became intoxicated.

It was the only place of amusement for the homeless youths of the town. There was not even a vestige of a library.

Early spring brought many changes. Tom returned from the Philippines. Out of his salary of thirteen dollars a month as a soldier, he had saved nearly one hundred dollars.

He gave Virginia twenty dollars and spent the rest of the money within a week.

"I got sick when I crossed the State line," he said, reeling with me from the bar of Coffee's Saloon.

He had become heavy-shouldered, with tousled red hair.

Like his Uncle Dennis before him, he walked westward one April morning and returned no more.

There was more evident in Tom the wild blood of the Lawlers. Incapable of restraint, he served half his army term in the guard house. But he had a superior strain. It was Tom who first gave me books to read in the orphanage. Through him I first learned about Napoleon and Alexander the Great. He early planted in my mind the seed of ambition. His knuckles were broken, his fingers twisted from many brawls.

He had the gift of phrase and the love of beauty. He could endure solitude. He ended, a gold prospector in Mexico.

After Tom had gone, Virginia cried for a few days as my mother had so long before when Dennis Lawler left.

"It's never to be—for I'm going away too—we're better off apart." All six of us had been together but one hour since our mother's death.

[255]

There followed an evening of weeping in the wretched home.

Then came Virginia's decision. She took her young sister and a tin trunk to Chicago.

I took to the road, the ring, and the jail.

CHAPTER XXII

A RENDEZVOUS FOR BEGGARS

VIRGINIA was more gypsy at heart than Irish. Her complexion was dark. Her eyes were a sad and misty blue.

Her new home in Chicago was a rendezvous for beggars. When she was not working or looking for work, she spent hours talking soothingly to bill collectors at the front door, and letting in beggars at the rear.

Her furniture was always bought on the installment plan. It was, whenever possible, of some design that could be turned into a bed by night. By morning all available sleeping places would be occupied. Homeless birds often slept upon the floor.

Virginia slept in a large Morris chair that opened like a jack-knife to form a cot.

She was short, quick and decisive of movement, and pensive. Her hair was chestnut and very long. At thirty, and in spite of having inherited the strength of many peasant ancestors, she was a physical wreck.

In time, after many, many days, she generally paid all her bills. If a collector were too stern, she would pawn another article, for which she had not yet paid. With the money obtained she would hold off the irate collector.

"I'd buy the sun for a candle if I could get it for fifty cents down," she used to say.

When desperately needing money for her many charities and bill collectors, she paid sixty dollars cash for a police dog puppy. All things were abused in this world, according to Virginia. She thought she saw a sad expression in the dog's eyes. She pawned a diamond ring, for which she had not paid, and bought the dog.

She wanted me to name the combination tiger and coyote, so I called him Jurgen.

Virginia knew the history of the gay pawnbroker.

"My brother, Jim, named him," she would often tell her gathering of derelicts.

The dog grew into a neighborhood terror.

No one could go near him except Virginia. She contended that he was really a gentle and misunderstood animal.

"Good Heavens," I once said to her, "why didn't you get a machine gun."

"I will when they sell them on time," she replied, with a smile.

Jurgen bit so many people that she was forced to move to another neighborhood.

He soon bit the lady who owned the new apartment.

The lady sued Virginia, and sought to prove that Jurgen had rabies. Virginia was forced to have the animal tested in a hospital. Not able to move right away, she sought to convince the bitten lady that Jurgen had died. It cost twenty-five dollars a week for Jurgen's hospital fees. Unable to bear the expense longer, she finally smuggled him up the back stairs one bitterly cold night. Ever afterward she kept him locked in a back bedroom.

Having won forty dollars at the races, she bought an expensive new hat. It was a dashing creation. She wore it home, where all the stray people admired it. She had actually paid twenty dollars down.

She laid it gently on the bed in the back room. She found a small feather and a smile on the face of Jurgen next morning.

As the dog grew older he became more set in his opinions.

One spring morning a colored ice man came up the back stairs. A large cake of ice was thrown across his shoulders. Jurgen jumped through a screen window at him. The negro swung the ice tongs in an agony of fear. They caught Jurgen under the throat. He went hurtling down five flights to his death. For fear the landlady would see him, Virginia gave Jurgen's assassin ten dollars to take his body away. She cried for several days over her misunderstood companion's sad end.

The people whom she sheltered often stole trifles from one another. They also stole from their hostess. She did not scold, but blamed herself for not locking things up securely. Often she would leave her apartment "on business." It consisted in walking rapidly to the park and watching children play. She loved grace in every variety. Never having learned to skate as a child, she would stand for an hour and watch boys and girls whirl about on the ice, their many colored mufflers swinging in wide circles as they skated.

After Virginia had worked for several months as a cashier in a cheap restaurant she decided to buy a vacant lot. The price was fifteen hundred dollars. Her salary was ten dollars a week. Immediately her mind was flooded with visions of wealth. "Russell Sage made a million in real estate," she would often say. She paid three hundred dollars at different periods on the lot. She sold her interest for a hundred dollars in order to pay Jurgen's hospital bill.

Grieved over the brute's death, she went to a town adjacent to Chicago and started a small lingerie store. Like her grandfather, Old Hughie Tully, she knew linens and laces at a glance. She stocked her store with articles of fine quality. She charged working girls exorbitant prices for them. The girls, in turn, bought on the installment plan. They failed to pay. In six months the would-be merchant was nearly penniless in Chicago again.

She carried about with her for years an iron statue of a gypsy. He was dressed in green trousers and red blouse. He poked at a fire with an iron rod. A red electric globe was concealed in an iron brush. Each night Virginia would turn all the lights out in the room, save the red flare under the gypsy. Often she would sit alone and gaze at the gypsy. She had never gone to school over two years in all. Her favorite reading were the great Russian realists. She could not spell three words in succession. In conversation she had poise and an instinctive ability to pronounce words correctly, or at least find simpler words with which to express herself.

The mystical sadness of her mother was ever with her.

She remained always a Catholic. When I tried to get behind her belief, to probe to the limit of her faith, she would always say:

"Well—it's a good show. It rests me, and I feel better when I go to church. Even if in the end I find out I'm wrong I'd still think it was wiser to kid myself."

She had many shabby love affairs. A tawdry array of men marched in and out of her heart. Each went his way, and left her stupefied for the next romance. At thirty-eight she said, "The prints of their shoes are all in my heart—" and then with a little gesture of defiance. "But I should give a damn."

CHAPTER XXIII

THE GIRL WHO WALKED WITH GOD

THERE was a young Irishman who found his way to Virginia's rendezvous.

He was stooped and cadaverous. He coughed and chewed gum. He continually rubbed a chin upon which hair would not grow. His face was long, pallor intense, his mouth drooped. He was slithery and gaunt with a lazy heart and an alert mind—when linen was discussed.

His father had been a linen mill superintendent in Belfast. His grandfather had worked in the same mill. His life had been devoted to the same commodity.

He sold linen over a counter at a large department store.

Each night he would talk to Virginia about linen. He would laugh at the ignorance of the American people concerning it.

Whenever a piece of linen had been mislaid

with no price tag, it was handed to Dunning. He would touch it with a wet thumb and forefinger, holding his chewing gum firmly between his teeth as he did so, as though long propinquity had made him contemptuous.

The linen which Dunning wore was always slightly soiled and in disarray.

He seldom talked to any one except Virginia. Each night regularly at nine he would prepare for bed. Before stretching out his long frame he would cough and say his prayers. He would then lie upon the bed, his hands folded across his chest like a gaunt Irish corpse ready for burial.

Morning would streak across his grisly bed and find him in the same position.

He would look at the yellow splotches on the faded red wall, then at the rough bricks of another building a few feet from his window—then rise and say his prayers.

Linen was the finest thing in life to Dunning. He gauged all things accordingly.

The owner of the store had "a cotton soul."

He became attached to Virginia—their love of linen being a common ground.

Dunning would get drunk every Saturday night. He would remain nearly unconscious in his room until time for late Mass on Sunday morning. He would then get ready for church with the same precision that he would sell a linen table cloth. In rainy, snowy or zero weather, he would walk down the Boulevard while the church bell tolled solemnly and slowly as if keeping time with his steps.

On Sunday evening he would often sit with Virginia in the living room and drink black coffee, with only the red light glowing under the iron gypsy.

Into these sessions there came from out of Ohio, one of the most beautiful of young women.

She had left her home at seventeen to travel with a cheap carnival company. Within a year she was known as the most beautiful girl in the Follies.

Her hair was dark, her eyes hazel, her features like those on a rare Grecian coin.

[266]

Newsboys on crowded city streets would stop to look at her.

Still a virgin, she came to Chicago when the company went on tour. She met a millionaire whom she learned to love, and to whom she surrendered after many months.

He cracked her life to pieces as a bullet would a delicate piece of pottery. She lived with him for a year, on the North Shore. Allowed fifty thousand dollars a year to spend, she was hated by her lover's shrew mother, and was at last abandoned by him.

Alone, she faced the wretched monotony of the dreary days.

By one of those accidents, which Virginia always considered a miracle, the girl found her way to her strange rendezvous.

Virginia was standing at her front door, when the girl passed on her way to look at a room on the floor above.

My mother's daughter was never quite of the city. She greeted the girl warmly.

The driving snow flurried down Washington Boulevard like feathers in a canyon gale. The girl, with the débris of her life in her eyes, told Virginia her errand.

Within a short time all arrangements were made for the girl to live with Virginia.

Deep in her heart my sister was of the opinion that all men were hyenas. She encouraged the girl to bring suit against the millionaire for one hundred thousand dollars.

The leading lawyer in Chicago was engaged.

In this way one of the most famous breach of promise suits in America was filed, from the rendezvous for beggars.

The girl's photograph adorned the front pages of the leading American newspapers.

A year passed. The girl hardly left the apartment. She sat as one bereft of life and hope. A beautiful fragment, she longed for motherhood and recoiled from men.

Her wealthy ex-lover was forced to pay twenty-five thousand dollars. Her share was sixteen thousand. She left the apartment as suddenly as she came.

Other derelicts abused the girl and accused

[268]

her of the common failing of all mankind—ingratitude.

Virginia's comment was, "I did nothing for her—it made me happy."

When the money was gone she returned destitute to Virginia. She was gladly welcomed. All were instructed to be especially kind to her.

And now with Virginia and the cadaverous linen seller, she gazed at the iron gypsy and his make-believe fire. . . .

The snow covered everything. From an alcove window Virginia gazed for a moment down the white boulevard.

"Isn't it beautiful?" she asked. "It reminds me of Grandad Tully's description of bleaching linen in Ireland."

She turned from the window. "He was like you, Dunning—

"He would talk by the hour about linen. I remember as a little girl he told me that people first learned to weave linen by watching birds build their nests. He told me how flax grew in fields like wheat—and how it was pulled up by the roots—a handful at a time.

[269]

"He said that linen cloth buried in tombs for thousands of years has been taken out good as new."

"That's true," said the linen salesman. "I've seen it stand washing and ironing."

The girl from the Follies looked more beautiful than ever in the dim light. She toyed with a small lace embroidered linen handkerchief.

"Gee—I love linen and silk," she said slowly. "I couldn't live without them."

The linen salesman looked at her with more interest.

An ambassador had fallen in love with her in New York.

She had told Virginia the story.

Feeling that the bird was captured, he furnished a beautiful cage for it.

The girl would not allow the naïve diplomat to touch her.

Dismayed at the strangeness of men, she left the apartment.

"Mr. —— could have bought you a ton of linen," Virginia said quickly.

The girl cupped her chin in a slender hand.

"I know—but I'd rather have cotton with some one I loved." She looked demurely at the Irish seller of linen,—and continued:

"I'm just made different, I guess, it may be a funny way to be made—but I can't help it."

The linen salesman took a stick of chewing gum from his vest pocket.

Virginia looked from one to the other.

She then went to the kitchen to prepare coffee.

The salesman moved closer to the girl.

"You're the kind of a girl I like," he finally commented, "one that's honest and true." He looked at her admiringly.

"Do you go to church?" he asked.

"Every Sunday—except in Lent—then I go three times a week," the girl replied.

"That's fine," was the rejoinder—"no woman ever went very far without religion."

"My mother always told me that—she used to say that if a girl walked with God the devil would never follow."

Silent moments passed.

[271]

Virginia returned with the coffee.

The linen salesman had a method of cheating his employers.

He stole several hundred dollars each week.

If a lady bought a hundred dollar linen table cloth Dunning would steal the receipt when it came from the wrapper.

He would steal a similar cloth the same day.

In a few days it would be brought to the refund desk by a confederate. That gentleman or lady would leave with a hundred dollars.

In time Dunning had saved five thousand. It was his intention to start an exclusive linen store.

In this he was frustrated. His employers, recognizing merit, sent him to Brussels as a linen buyer at twelve thousand a year.

He left with the girl from the Follies.

CHAPTER XXIV

POOR KATH-U-RINE

My grandfather's nature was often serene and beautiful as heather in the sun. It could instantly become hard as a horse's hoof.

In long and far wandering I recall no other men who more definitely saw with their own eyes and followed their own instincts than my father and his sardonic witty sire. It never occurred to them to apologize for any failings which others thought they had. They walked as unconcernedly down their chaotic roads of life as two lions through a moonlit jungle.

Uncouth, even barbaric, their intelligence was never satisfied, always were they alert to life. They seem to me, even yet, like spectators drinking at a bar between the acts of a comedy.

At times my grandfather would swear slightly at the obscurity of his life and the narrowness of his sphere. His tantrum at fate would pass in an instant.

There was, at the back of his huge head, the feeling that he was a great politician who never had a chance.

He was always at the cross-roads of gayety and sadness. He never took the sad road so long as a drink was at hand.

If the hours hung heavy, as they often did in a small town, he would sit tilted back in his chair against the wall of a saloon, and hum a weird tune, which he often chanted with that strange gift of the Irish—the blending of tears with hilarity. But now he had the abstract manner of a man whose mind was far away.

The words, like the memory of old Hughie Tully, are still with me—

> *"I'm very happy where I am,*
> *Far across the say,*
> *I'm very happy far from home,*
> *In North Amerikay.*
>
> *"It's lovely in the night when Pat*
> *Is sleepin' by my side,*

I lie awake, and no one knows
The big tears that I've cried;"

As if hiding tenderness, the old man would look sternly about the saloon.

"*For a little voice still called me back*
To my far, far counthrie,
And nobody can hear it spake,
Oh! nobody but me.

"*There is a little spot of ground*
Behind the chapel wall,
It's nothing but a tiny mound,
Without a stone at all;

"*It rises like my heart jist now,*
It makes a little hill;
It's from below the voice comes out,
I cannot kape it still.

"*Oh! little voice; ye call me back*
To my far, far counthrie,

[275]

And nobody can hear ye spake,
Oh! nobody but me."

"Ho, ho, ho!" he once ejaculated, with a look of contempt when he had finished the words—"the likes ov a big man like me chantin' sich rubbish—it's like staylin' a baby's candy on Christmas mornin'!"

"When did you learn it, Grandaddy?" I asked him.

"I picked it up in a dhrunken moment frim yere grandmither—she's full ov sich swatemates."

I had never defended my grandmother before. To me she had always been tender, her voice ever a croon.

"I like grandmother—" I said impulsively— "I think she's smarter'n—," I stopped with my grandfather's steel eyes narrowed at me.

"Yis, yis, smarter then me—niver sthop— say yere say—spake it out," he said tersely.

He paused. His eyes went softer.

"Yere grandmither—but no one should talk about a good woman—it's the other kind that

[276]

make the good stories—an' I'm an ould man."

He became more pensive.

His fingers drummed on his knee.

"I wondher where John Crasby is—all day I've not seen his long shadow."

He half smiled and hummed—

"I came from Alabama
Wid my banjo on my knee;
I' gwine to Louisiana,
My true love for to see.
It rained all night the day I left,
The weather it was dry,
The sun so hot I froze to death:
Susanna, don't you cry.

"O! Susanna, O! don't you cry for me;
I've come from Alabama
Wid my banjo on my knee.

"So ye sthick up for yere grandmither," he said sternly—and stopped. "Well it's right ye should—it's nayther human nor crayture did she iver harm—I seen her nurse a wild rabbit in

[277]

Ireland—an' close its eyes in the ind as if it were St. Pathrick.

"There's more in a woman's heart, me boy, then the Holy Mither Church kin iver git out.

"Yere grandmither is pure Irish—an' not like us—crossed wit' wind-rovin' Danes—an' there's a lot o' sins the Danes must answer for— the Irish were goin' along paceful sometimes wit' their own good dhrinks—an' then the Danes came an' taught 'em to make beer out ov heather—it tashted like rain water an' soap in a can—but the Irish—thim ov the weak minds would git dhrunk on the stuff—"

He paused, his face wrinkled in disgust.

"Ireland had a big navy—it was so big the admirals were common sailors—they could ate Inglind for breakfast before the Danes got thim to dhrinkin' beer—thin came the ind—it wasn't long before they begin rubbin' their hands an' bowin' whin the King passed by to kape a date wit' a bawdy woman—

" 'What strange payple,' said the king, 'they bow an' they scrape before me who am not ov their blood—'

[278]

" 'Ah, don't you understhand,' says a fierce lookin' Dane—wit' hair longer an' redder then yere mither's—'Yere scarlet Majesty,' says he —'we give them beer to dhrink'—

"An' the king's royal fat sides wint thin with laughin'.

" 'What a joke to phlay on sthrong min,' says he—'it's like fadin' crame to tigars and makin' em purr—. I ain't had sich a good laugh since the time I killed me royal father' says he—thin he rose to his four feet four—an' scratched the sores on his royal face.

" 'Bring the man before me who invinted givin' the Irish beer," commands he.

"They brought before the king a shrivelled up Dane from whose hands dript blood. They looked like claws.

"A man behind him whispered—'They got that way your precious Majesty from chokin' Irish babies for Cromwell.'

" 'Shut up,' growled the king—'It is beer an' not blood of which we talk.'

"The beer invinter only had one eye an' it

[279]

was at the ind ov his nose—there were siven
strakes ov blood across it—an' it nary moved—
like the eye ov a dead fish—it was his lip hung
low, an' was heavy like liver.

" 'What a bea-utiful lip,' says the king—
'an' what a nice sad eye he has—'

" 'Eye ever faithful to the service of any
king,' says the beer invinter.

" 'A Dane who should be Irish,' says the
king—'he'll serve anybody.'

" '*Anybody*,' says the beer invinter with the
bloody strames across his eyes—'I've been in
Ireland long enough to learn obaydience.'

" 'Of sich is the kingdom of kings,' says the
king—may God in His divine wisdom kape yere
heart pure,' says he.

"The king scratched his royal sores, an'
looked at the invinter ov beer.

" 'What a handsome man you are,' says he
—'how ilegant—an' what be-utiful hands you
have wit' their fine red color—it's like the sun
glimmerin' on me palace walls—

" 'Even without a cint in yere pocket ye

should climb far on the ladder ov glory,' says the king—'yere hands are bint so as to hold the ropes—

" 'I'll make ye the Right Rivrind Royal Climber,' says his royalty—'an' ye kin test the ropes ov the doomed that are brave enough to bethray me—ye shall soak the ropes in beer that the odor ov thim may help to kill traitors—'

"He kissed the man above the eye—

" 'Blissed be anither Royal Knight,' says he—'Rope Tester and Beer Taster to the King —in all his terrible dominions.' He pinned a lot ov badges on the monster Dane—an' he slunk from the sight of men wit' 'em rattlin' on his breast."

Old Hughie rubbed his forehead.

"But all that has nothin' to do wit' yere grandmither."

His voice became lighter.

"If I do be tellin' ye—she was beautiful as the moon over Killarney when the sthars are dim. Her father was—Squire Byrne—he was considerable of a man—he was—but it's not

[281]

who yere father was—except that if the
father's a woman the daughter will be aven
less—

"A man smashed out of rock he was—silent
as the bog—an' sthrong as the wind on the
ocean—he was like me own father—no pain
iver bint him—Both of thim wint to the
meadow ov the dead sudden—they're taythe
still sthrong enough to ate the bones ov the
dead."

He looked about the saloon as if fearful that
someone would hear.

"Yere grandmither is like him. The yares
have come on her soft as the dew on grass.
She's phroud as Lucifer on Sunday morning.

"Some people grow old like a withered
quince—an' others like a big ripe apple in the
sun—yere grandmither's like that. An' let no
one tell ye, me boy, that yere grandmither has
no nerve. One time, whin yere father was a
baby he was about to die ov the closin ov the
lungs. An' the doctor came into the room an
says, 'I'm sorry—but it's only a few hours now

—at the most. Is the baby baptized,' he says. 'That'll keep it outta limbo—an' its only right that sich a baby should not be forever in sich a dark place—but see the face of God.' Yere grandmither looked at yere poor father thin a few months old, an' she says to the doctor—'Be gone with ye, sir, over the road through the bog, 'tis no man from the big college who kin tell me a baby's dead before it isn't.' She took onions and fried 'em in grease from the pet goose, an' she wrapped yere father up in it." The old man chuckled. "An' she saved ye're father's life—an' played a joke on ye, my boy."

"No heart-bitter wound would she iver show—aven if it killed her—

"She scholded me often for the dhrink—and has these fifty gone years—as she should—an' knowin' love as I do to be a paradise for fools that niver kin be—I'd marry her agin tomorrow —if she were brave enough to face the long throuble agin—"

He sighed deeply—

"It's no wonder she wrote jingles—livin' wit' the likes ov me—

"Wit' a heart bolder then murdher, her duty made her swate like a child—

"Poor Kath-u-rine!!"

CHAPTER XXV

BOTTOMS UP FOR OLD HUGHIE

RHEUMATISM crawled like a torpid river toward Old Hughie Tully's heart.

"Indade," he would clutch his breast, "the rist o' me's good, but here I am playin' tag wit' the grave."

A crucifix hung above his bed. Upon it was a plaster Christ with one arm and a broken foot. Old Hughie looked at the broken Christ.

"Oh, well—he died too," he turned his heavy face away.

"But he come to life agin—so they say."

Grandmother walked in and out of the room, as silent as a broken shadow on a grave.

She was bent nearly double in the vise of age. She held a corn cob pipe between thin tight lips and toothless gums.

Half her aged life was spent in keeping her pipe lit. On and on she would chatter in a ceaseless mirage of Irish nothings. She would then relight her pipe.

Now her pipe remained unlit.

Her lips seldom opened.

A once heavy woman, she had shrivelled to less than eighty pounds. Freckles dotted the edges of her deep wrinkles. Her heart had grown sweet in grief. Her soul remained strong with the years.

She was older than my grandfather.

An unyielding woman, the passion of her life had been Old Hughie and my father.

With that pathetic scuttering away from reality which is too typical of America I was early told of my grandmother's high breeding.

She claimed that she could trail her ancestry to the Spanish Celts who colonized Ireland hundreds of years before the coming of Christ. Old Hughie, at heart, thought little of grandmother's lineage. "We all come from somebody—and I came as far Kathurin—why it was one ov me own great grandfather's that dug the ditch that run through Rome."

But the illusion of her great learning was

[286]

ever with my father. "If ye inherited anything from anybody, Jim, it was from your grand-mither—she was an educated woman."

Always was she asking Old Hughie now, "can I do anything for ye Hughie?"

The kindly old despot would answer each time, "No Kath-u-rin—thanks be."

She would look for a moment at the immense head of her master, buried in the pillow. Her mouth would contract and tremble at the edges. It would then become tight as she hobbled from the room.

"Poor Kath-u-rin," murmured Hughie to John Crasby as he entered the room, "she'll kill me wit' kindness."

The men looked at each other. Crasby's hand raised. "It's all right, Hughie."

"Shure—an' it's all right—why wouldn't it be . . indade an' I'll pour beer over the lilies on your grave."

"Sure you will," returned Crasby, "well I know it."

He stood in the center of the room.

Old Hughie looked at him with narrow eyes.

[287]

"How's the wither out, John?"

"Very good Hughie—we'll be takin' a walk tomorrow."

"Not me John—niver no more—"

He looked up at the broken Christ.

"It's a ride I'll be takin.'" He pulled his arm from beneath the quilt, "To the cimetary —God help me. . ."

"You mustn't talk like that Hughie," Crasby's voice was whisky cracked and soft, "you're good for many the year yet."

"But not here John—out in the grave." He looked keenly at Crasby again. "An' ye'll be braggin' how ye put me there—whin ye know that no man kin do that."

John Crasby moved closer to the bed. A one time dandy, tall, with a long red nose, and nearly hairless head, he rubbed his thin throat.

"I'll be goin' ahead of you, Hughie, I'm seventy-three—no more signs to paint—no more work an' no more drinkin'—nothin'—"

Crasby looked around the room. "But I give you my word, Hughie—I'll tell 'em up town it's the rheumatiz what's wrong with you—and I'll tell 'em all you said hello—"

"Shure—an' do that, John—I'll not say it often any more."

"An' I'll tell 'em you'll be up an' around by Sunday, Hughie," Crasby added cheerfully.

"An' ye won't brag if I go—will ye John—for remimber—it's hard enough to lave—without that—" The last words fell into a whisper. "It's not much to ask ye, John," he added slowly, "but ivery man has his pride."

Crasby held out a long arm.

"Hughie—if I iver say a word you can ha'nt me. May I drink your ghost in ivery glass if I iver betray any word—but you're not going—ye old baby—we'll both live to drink fifty one-legged men under the table."

Old Hughie smiled at the memory.

Late that afternoon Old Hughie Tully died.

My father followed my grandmother into the room.

They looked at the shaggy old man for a long time.

[289]

Sorrow was never endured with greater dignity.

For more than fifty married years my grandmother had stood by Old Hughie. It was said by some that as a ten year old girl she had taught him to walk.

"Well, Hughie's gone," she said at last to my father. Her pipe fell to the floor. "Blissed Jasus have mercy."

My father said nothing. He took his mother from the room.

The one negro in the town attended his funeral.

The priest said a few commonplace words over him.

Jack Raley and John Crasby did not go into the church.

In Mahon's saloon all drinking was suspended for one minute.

"That's long enough to hold your drinks, men—Hughie himself would have you hold them no longer—" he lifted his glass—All followed him. "It's bottoms up for Old Hughie."

Many voices chanted—"Bottoms up for Old Hughie."

* * * * * * *

He lay in his yellow oak coffin, his gnarled hands folded on his broad chest, his head tilted back as if for a drink.

Saloon keepers and bartenders looked out of front doors along Spring Street as the funeral passed.

* * * * * * *

John Crasby was the last to leave Mahon's saloon that night. The roosters crowed as he walked, bottle in pocket, toward the cemetery.

With unsteady gait he made his way to Old Hughie's grave. He seated himself upon the newly upturned earth. He took the bottle and a small glass from his coat pocket. He filled the glass and held it so the moon's rays slanted across the red liquor. He looked carefully at the grave.

"Your head would be about here, Hughie— this'll soak down your throat."

He poured the liquor on the ground.

"There's one for you, Hughie."

He filled the glass and drained it.

"Here's one for me."

"One more for you Hughie," he poured again.

"Here's one for me." He drank.

Glass after glass was emptied in this way. The bottle empty, he stood it upside down on the whisky-soaked earth.

For a long time he stared at the vastness of the midnight sky.

Rising unsteadily, he hiccoughed,

"G'by—Hu-gh-ie," and staggered home.